UNDER HIS KILT

MELISSA BLUE

Confessions of a Romance Author

Under His Kilt by Melissa Blue

This is a work of fiction. Names, characters, places, and incidents are either the product of the author's imagination or are used fictitiously, and any resemblance to actual persons living or dead, business establishments, events, or locales, is entirely coincidental.

Cover Art by Melissa Blue
Self-Published Edition 2013
ISBN-10: 1511803177

Also by Melissa Blue

Under The Kilt

Under His Kilt
Her Insatiable Scot
Kilted For Pleasure

Down With Cupid Shorts

Weekend Lover
Down With Cupid
Betting It All

Den of Sin

Forbidden Rendezvous
Debauching the Virgin
Unbidden Desires

MELISSA BLUE

UNDER HIS KILT

Jocelyn Pearson is determined to spend her last month as a twenty-something doing everything she's too busy or scared to try. Her imagination runs wild and then fixates on Ian Baird. He'll be working at the Langston Museum for a short stint as a consulting curator. He's Scottish. He believes sex is fun to be had. He's the perfect choice for a fling. She only has to get him break his rule about sleeping with co-workers. Seducing a man was on her bucket list...

Ian is no one's fool and knows exactly what Jocelyn wants—him. If she didn't work for the Langston Museum, he'd be more than happy to oblige any and every fantasy she desired, but she's the curator. She's sweet, inexperienced and well liked by everyone including the museum owner and director. Ian can't risk losing such an important contact for his consulting business. Not even when everything within in him craves a taste of her.

When Jocelyn sets her sights on him, there's no way Ian can deny her. They agree their affair will end in thirty days. No emotions, no entanglements, just sex. The closer the end date looms, they start to question if it's possible to walk away. They'll either have to come to terms of what they've become or stick to their original agreement.

CHAPTER ONE

"Not one kilt anywhere?" Flabbergasted by this notion, Jocelyn Pearson stared at Ian Baird. Her *sort of* boss stood across the museum's expansive storage basement. She tried to wrap her mind around the busted myth and couldn't.

"When I think of Scotland," she continued, "I imagine men wear kilts like men in America wear jeans. Casual. No muss. No fuss."

Her ramble teased a smile out of Ian and put another crack in his impenetrable façade. She held her breath for a three count and let it out slowly to contain the primitive surge of attraction. A month and still that simple facial tick made her want to launch herself at him.

Big wooden crates filled the dark room below the small museum. The crates separated them, but didn't seem like much of an obstacle when all she wanted was to close the distance.

"I'm not saying you can't find one." The sensuous curve of his lips could have tempted a saint. "It's just not everyday wear. Before you ask, we also wear boxers when we do."

His words implied he'd worn a kilt.

Oh, God.

Ian in a kilt...drool. Her skin tightened and flushed beneath her soft cotton dress shirt. She'd never seen him out of his uniform of slate gray slacks, dark suit jacket, white dress shirt and black tie. The expensive silk clung to thick, sculpted muscles, but she couldn't help but picture him in a Cameron Clan plaid. Absolutely commando—no matter what he said—just waiting for the right breeze to lift up the material and expose just a bit more of him.

She balled her hands. Her fingertips itched to trace the seam of his mouth. "Next you're going to tell me there's no Santa or Easter Bunny."

His blue-gray irises darkened and his nostrils flared. "Aye. Your parents lied. Those fuckers don't exist." He spoke low, husky with just a hint of a Scottish burr.

Her high heels rasped over the concrete floor as she shifted another step *from* him. "Good, because I planned to be naughty this year."

Tension rippled through his frame. No doubt with the coil of muscles that made up his sleek physique he could have vaulted over the row of crates if he wanted to. "You? Naughty? Aye, right."

She liked that they'd built up a rapport, and because they had, Jocelyn grinned at his perplexed expression from her announcement. "Aye. Naughty. Me."

He grunted out a soft tut. "Not like 'oy.' You're not hurting. Just say 'I' like *I* went to the shop."

She tried again. Her effort to infuse a false burr coaxed out his low rumble of laughter. "Good, Lass."

His accent only thickened the few times she'd seen him frustrated. So she smiled at his teasing. His brow lifted but he flipped through the inventory list. That action reminded her why they were there. Her job involved ensuring he was satisfied with every last detail—from receiving the shipment to the display in the small Californian museum.

The responsibilities included having the right security, lighting and placement for the priceless objects when the Langston Museum had its unveiling in four weeks. Ian, the head of the traveling exhibit, had to ensure everything displayed was authentic, in one piece and stayed that way until shipped to the next destination. That made him her boss, of sorts, as liaison to the Langston and his pet project.

He inspired the kind of fantasies that she wished... Fixing her mind back on work, Jocelyn dropped the subject. The shipment had come in late and it would be a long work night, not one filled with what ifs.

"Naughty?" he asked, circling back to a topic she assumed he'd left alone.

Caught off guard, she blurted out, "Um, I'm twenty-nine."

His gaze lifted from the paperwork, and he waited silently for her to explain the tangent. She added, "I'll be thirty on the day of the opening."

She blew out a breath and tried to explain her current insanity. "There's a lot I haven't done and I plan to do it this year. Consider it my mid-life crisis. I'm thinking of all the things I should have experienced by now, and looking down the barrel of thirty, I damn well plan to do them."

He made a soft sound. "Like?"

"Drink the worm in the tequila bottle," she said.

"Why?" he asked, sounding confused.

She'd spent the previous ten years getting the right degrees, the right internships, jobs and contacts. She didn't have a moment to take a step back and live. Every single one of those moments had been spent getting her here.

Maybe in a year or two she'd get a chance to travel but

she couldn't wait another moment to...let loose for a little while. She felt brittle and old already. All she needed were pearls, a cardigan sweater and a knitting circle of friends.

But, Ian hadn't asked for all that. "What did you do on your 21st birthday?"

His head tilted back and a glint shone in his gaze. "Don't remember most of it."

"Exactly," she said with barely contained excitement. "Plan to do the same kind of celebrating for my thirtieth."

"It's not so bad," he muttered.

She frowned. "Excuse me?"

"Turning thirty isn't so bad."

He didn't look that much older than her, but she inspected him for any real tells of age. Laugh lines grooved along the skin around his mouth. Lush black strands curled around the collar of his suit jacket. Not a gray hair to speak of. He couldn't be that much older, but she couldn't tell at a glance. He had a poise that made him seem mature, earthy.

She pursed her lips. "Still, I'm planning to ring it in with a bang."

His gaze met hers for another tense moment. The hairs at the nape of her neck rose and her breathing deepened. His hand tightened on the clipboard, but he made a noncommittal noise and focused on the list again.

Jocelyn blinked. No, she hadn't imagined that moment, but she ignored the tension pregnant with possibility. Nothing should or would break through the invisible and unspoken boundary they'd drawn up weeks ago. A boundary that wavered with just a heated glance.

Finally, he handed her the clipboard. "All there?" she asked.

"Nothing out of place. Let's work our way from the back to the front." Ian picked up the crowbar from a table covered with other tools without losing stride.

He stopped at the first lot taken off the truck, put down the crowbar and began to loosen his tie and jacket. He flipped up the sleeves of his shirt and rolled them up his forearms. Yup, bronzed skin. Miles worth of golden skin tanned, not from any Scottish sun but from his travels around the world. Sinew. Sexy. Yup, she had to grip the clipboard and hope that would be enough to rein in the urge to jump him.

"What's first on your list?" he asked.

Find a lover. Preferably someone with a Scottish accent. "I've never had a drunken Karaoke night," she said without a hitch in her voice.

"The key is getting as wrecked as possible. Otherwise, it's not half as fun." With expertise and precision, he pried off the nailed-down lid. "Read it off."

She told him what should be in there; he nodded and put the top back on. "And then?" She looked down at the clipboard and he tutted. "Your list," he said.

Have my lover do everything I couldn't think to ask for. "Skydiving."

"Exhilarating," he said.

They followed the same process of him opening the lid and having her read off the clipboard. He had some opinion to give on everything else on her personal list. So much so, Jocelyn wondered how he'd react if she blurted out, "have sex with you," but then her palms dampened more. That would be insane, impulsive, passionate...everything she'd never been.

Chuck it all. Blurt it out. She considered the words, bit

her lip for a second and then asked, "What haven't you done?"

And then he smiled again—the one that made her panties wet and had her one step away from throwing herself at him.

"A gentleman never tells."

Oh. Oh. She had to *know*. And it wasn't her imagination that could see he wanted to tell her what a gentleman should never repeat.

*****

"Uh—um." Jocelyn cleared her throat and the soft sound feathered over Ian's senses. "You always answer my questions."

"I do," he agreed but didn't elaborate. The storage room held a chill. Her nipples beaded against the starched-white shirt. He blew out the breath he'd been holding.

"Why stop now?"

Because he'd been listening for it, Ian heard the unfettered passion in her voice and that right there was why—self-preservation. "Some things you don't share with a lady." He paused and then smiled. "Unless you're about to do those same things to her."

Her skin, a shade of the darkest honey he'd ever seen, flushed. She bit down on her lip and broke the gaze. "That's fair."

And that's why he hadn't touched her. She was innocent in all the ways he'd ruin. But, Joce...had a way about her. Sharp and a little stubborn. That keen gaze was on him now, drinking in his every movement. The past few weeks it had grown harder to ignore the unquenchable desire he saw there. Younger, dumber and having been raised in a bachelor pad, Ian wouldn't have cared. He'd have made it his mission to see how much it took to sate her. He'd since learned fucking coworkers always ended badly.

Ian leveled a look at her and reconsidered his rule. Thick ebony strands were twisted into a bun. The upswept hairdo only highlighted her almond-shaped eyes, dark chocolate irises and long lashes. She leaned forward checking the packaging tags. Smooth, delectable skin peeked out.

She looked prim in the pin-striped dress suit. Her tits high and tight. Unbelievably curvaceous hips made his fingers twitch. He wanted to sink his nails into them. She barely came up to his chin, but the cut of the skirt and high heels made her legs seem to go on forever. Prim and corruptible.

Always put together neatly, polite and personable...he was tempted to witness her stripped bare in a literal and figurative sense. He'd never fucked at work, but Ian thought about doing it now. The unruly consideration started a delicious pull on his balls that only feminine caresses and tender tugs could ease.

Her hands tightened on the clipboard and she brought it closer to her chest. Maybe she could see all that in his gaze. No matter how much he wanted to see her head thrown back, hair gripped in his fist and arse arched high, he couldn't. Not with her. She wasn't *sweet* but close enough to make things difficult.

"Next item?" he asked and ignored the tug.

She told him, her voice breathless, but he ignored the change in tone too.

"Technically," she said, "it wouldn't be kissing and telling if you haven't done it yet."

He laughed. "There's not much I haven't."

She tried to hide her chagrin by looking down, but he'd seen it. "Uh, public place seems too easy for you. What else?"

"Sex swing. Airplane." He gauged her reaction.

Her head snapped up. She swallowed. "Airplane. Bathroom's too small."

Fuck. "Noted," he said.

He lowered his gaze and worked up and down the room, letting her call off the lots. He didn't ask any more personal questions about what she hadn't done yet, especially in the bedroom. That way he wouldn't think about all the ways he'd like to do them with her.

It took them another hour to finish so by the time they entered the break room, they were the only ones left at work outside of security. The large room was well lit even with the cafes and bistros closed. They stood closer to the industrial-sized glass refrigerator, sink and microwave than to the central area with all the tables. In the quiet, with her, the moment felt strangely intimate.

"Thinking I'm going to call it a night, get up early tomorrow and finish the rest." She eased them into a conversation. "Then have a normal weekend."

She rested against the counter and blew into the hot coffee. The way her plump lips pursed shot straight to his dick. He sipped his drink silently, trying not to envision those same lips wrapped around the tip of his cock, wet and eagerly suckling him.

But he couldn't abide the uncomfortable silence, not with her. Joce would find some way to question him about something else if he left it. "When do you plan to start the insanity?"

"After work tomorrow."

He chuckled at the straight-forward admission. Finishing off the coffee, he put the cup in the sink. She'd closed her eyes, let her head fall back, exposing the beautiful curve of her neck.

He stilled, tried to breathe through the urge to taste her skin. "Heading out for drunken karaoke?"

Her eyes shot open and her gaze whipped to him, but then she smiled and it was one hundred percent mischievous. "No." She shook her head, the smile fading. "I probably shouldn't tell you this."

He wanted to see the smile cross her face again. "Then maybe you absolutely should."

She laughed, shook her head. "Can't believe I'm going to say this..." She sighed. "I'm going to pick up a guy in a bar. Never done that."

His gut clenched. Another man would do all the things he'd been imagining. She'd let him, because there were things she'd never done. Ian set his cup in the sink, keeping his hands to himself. "Shouldn't take you long, but I'd be careful if I were you."

"Careful? That's the whole point. I've lived my life pretty risk-free. I'm not saying I'm going to lose my mind, but I'm tired of doing the safe thing, the right thing. I want fun, reckless and maybe a little stupid. Break the rules I've made for myself."

He grappled onto his skewed moral code as her tongue glided over her bottom lip, lapping up every drop of warm liquid that clung to the flesh.

He flexed his fingers. "We'd be barbarians without rules."

Her brows furrowed. "Didn't take you for a rule

follower."

"I have my own," he said.

Her teeth grazed nervously over her bottom lip. He couldn't remember which rule kept him from reaching forward, or why it was important in the first place.

"I'm curious but I don't want to pry," she said.

So polite. Only a twisted son of a bitch would want to change that about her, to push just to see how she'd react. He had to say something to knock that unquenchable desire from her gaze. "What you're looking for, Sweetheart, you can't find in a bar hook-up."

"And what is it I'm looking for, Ian?"

"To be fucked senseless and not have a shred of guilt over it." He'd expected shock, a flush, anything other than the smile that started in the corner of her mouth and lit up her eyes.

"Yeah. Pretty much that."

The brazen confession made him laugh, made his cock rock hard. "All this time with you and I thought you were innocent."

"Nah." She shrugged. "Lost that sophomore year in high school."

Without thought he edged closer to her. Shit. He couldn't exactly wish her good luck, but he had to end this exchange before he changed his mind. He had no claim on her and shouldn't want one. He pushed off the counter. "Happy hunting. In the morning then?"

"You'll be here?" There was no mistaking the anticipation in her tone.

Ian smiled when he should have discouraged the emotion with a grave frown. "Aye."

He escaped with his dick still safely, smartly, in his

trousers. He'd call it a win.

CHAPTER TWO

Jocelyn spent most of her morning trying to talk herself out of adding a new item to her list of things to do before thirty—sex with Ian. The idea plagued her most of the night when they'd worked together, in the break room and in her bed as she tried to sleep. And now, early afternoon, she'd given up the useless litany of reasons why she shouldn't, how she wasn't the kind of woman who'd ask for sex. Women who had sex with Ian probably didn't ever ask politely for a roll in the sheets.

What could she do? She'd never seduced a man. And what about his rules? He hadn't needed to say sleeping with people at work was one of them. If they'd met in any other way there was no doubt in Jocelyn's mind he'd have ripped off her clothes, pinned her to the floor and screwed her every which way but loose.

And she would have let him.

Completely out of the norm for her, but she *had* to figure out a way to talk him into breaking his personal commandment, because she wanted him to pin her to the floor, wall, mattress, wherever and whenever. No use in lying about it or telling herself she shouldn't. That was the whole point behind the plan to do all the daring things she'd never done before. Good God, sitting here quietly helping him, paralyzed with what to do next, just solidified the fear that even at twenty-nine she'd lost all possible gumption and was slowly calcifying into a sexless, lonely, cardigan-wearing nun.

No. Hell no.

"You," Ian said, breaking her out of her reverie, "have been thinking furiously all morning. It's distracting."

He'd shed his coat and tie again today. Also, he'd rolled up his sleeves and smelled like something she wanted to swallow whole. *That* was distracting. She opened her mouth to let those words tumble out, but he looked up, gaze narrowing on her face.

"Scared of your plans after work?"

"You're teasing me," she said.

"I am."

She smiled despite the irritation of him, of all people, was poking fun at her staid life. *He* was the abnormal one. "Not everyone has arm-wrestled a shaman and won."

And then a thought struck her sideways. A man who'd done all the things Ian had probably didn't need much goading to do what he clearly already wanted to do. All those moments where he'd been one muscle twitch from jumping her hadn't been in her imagination. They both kept that boundary in place. What would happen if she tore it away? Ian couldn't cross a line that didn't exist. He'd built his career by being smart, courageous and certain. Not much changed his mind unless he wanted to be persuaded. And Ian wanted her. She was sure of it.

The thought sunk its teeth in. Her skin flushed and she did her best not to glance up with a grin that would look as mischievous as she felt. No, what she'd do next wasn't world domination. She just needed to make Ian lose control and break his goddamn rule. One, it seemed, he wanted to break anyway.

"I don't know what to do," she said, trying for sex kitten and not sure if it was working. "What makes you pick up a woman in a bar?"

His white-gloved hands froze over the ritual ax, and something passed behind his gaze she couldn't describe much less distill into a single word. "She's attractive and breathing."

She snorted and lost the hold on her sex kitten. "No really."

He considered her again, sighing. "Do you plan to walk up to him?"

"Exactly."

"Well, start with your walk. More leg and hip action. Not like those models who trot like horses. Sensual. Seductive. Understated. The kind of sway a man can imagine you being on top of him moving the same way."

With a sly smile she stood. His gaze narrowed on her. She scrounged up every thought of being on top of a man, his cock sliding in and out, how it would feel rising up and down, his fingers gliding over her waist, up to her breasts and fixed those thoughts in her mind and walked toward him. She stopped a few feet from him and raised a brow. "Like that?"

His hands gripped the ax. "Passable, but now put that movement into thought and there in your gaze."

She thought of Ian's fingers digging into her waist and holding her still so he could thrust into her. "Passable?"

He made a noncommittal noise. "Just like that, Lass."

But he wasn't joking when he said it this time. Not with the way he spoke so softly, but a bit of a growl could be heard in the back of his throat. Her nipples hardened as though his voice was something tangible and could scrape against the sensitive tips. She had to swallow. "And then what?"

"He'll do the rest of what needs to be doing to get you in his bed. No question." He flexed his fingers over the ax, his breathing uneven.

But he didn't move toward her, not even a twitch. She'd crossed the line they'd put up. Made it clear she wanted more to happen, and he wasn't doing what needed to be done to get her into his bed. *Damn.* Her gamble didn't work. She started to turn away so he wouldn't see the defeat creeping over her expression, but Ian spoke.

"But it's me you want, isn't it?"

Her steps froze at his words, but a corner of her mouth crooked up. "Depends." She faced him fully and saw he'd put down the ax.

"On what?"

"Whether or not you'll break your rule."

"And what rule would that be?" He stalked forward, to her.

Her heart jumped in her chest. "I assume it's something along the lines of you don't sleep with coworkers."

"A rule for a good reason, too."

"Complications," she said. "Sour grapes. Anything awkward if the sex isn't good or too good and one side buys into an emotional entanglement you don't want."

"Took the words out of my mouth. So, I'll say this once and I want you to believe it, down to your toes." He made another predatory step toward her. "I want to fuck you. Not make love or anything else with flower-y intent. No. *Fuck*. The kind that's sweat and come soaked and breaks some furniture in the process."

His words gave her pause, mainly because she had a visceral reaction to them, to him—wet. She was soaking wet and from the sudden jump in her heart rate, her hands trembled too. She'd had the hearts, the flowers and sweetly whispered words before. Great, wonderful even. Making love was like meat and potatoes—fulfilling and warm and right with the *right* person.

What Ian offered was sinful, decadent like something sweet, and then covered in chocolate just to make it that much better. Nothing that could sustain you, but by God, it was delicious and mouthwatering. The kind of sex that left you raw on the inside and out. Something she'd never had and it was about time she did.

"Am I supposed to be scared right now?"

He chuckled and it sounded like trouble—some she'd borrowed for no reason other than temporary insanity.

"Aye. But you teased me so I'm going to let you stew for a while until we finish up, and then we'll head to my place. You have until then to back out."

Maybe she should have been worried there was an escape-for-your life-while-you-can clause. She wanted something that would eclipse the first twenty-nine years of her life and make it seem like she hadn't even started yet. An experience that said tame and tasteful sex wasn't all there was to life.

So, she said. "Ditto, Ian."

He chuckled again and walked back to the ax. They went through everything, prepping as though nothing had changed. Really, that's what made her eventually start to quake in her heels. A man that didn't have to prove himself was a dangerous kind of man.

She couldn't wait.

CHAPTER THREE

Jocelyn assumed Ian lived in a home she could never afford on her current salary. Not that the museum paid her so little. She had a decent cushion of savings thanks to them.

Decent and opulent were worlds apart. He lived in a high-rise—the penthouse. He didn't make an over-the-top gesture when he opened the door to prepare her, but he should have.

"You live here?" She tried not to gape.

"Don't own it, but it's serviceable."

She worked with antiques and things that required countries to sign over and create contracts to lend to other places. But, this...wow.

"You're looking scared again, Joce."

She shook her head. "I know you're...important, but I didn't know how much. This place makes that pretty clear."

He frowned at the apartment, maybe seeing it through her eyes. The living room and kitchen had things you needed for functionality, but both had plenty of pretty things, breakable and costly. She kicked off her shoes only to have her feet sink into plush carpet.

"People pay to have things they don't need. To have a status that means nothing. Here, I can make what I need to eat or order it. I have a soft place to lay my head. The museum felt *this* is what I wanted."

He shrugged out of his coat and kept moving deeper into the high-rise. She followed because this was his domain and, to be honest, she'd handed over the reins to him. He knew what fucking was.

They passed by an original Van Gogh in the hallway and she almost stopped to admire it, but he kept going. "You don't care for all this?"

He halted, pushed open a door—his bedroom. "Not really. It's not home. It is what it is."

She'd noticed he preferred sparse in most things, but his clothes, for one, were tailored. He drove a high-end sports car and even lunch was ordered from nice places. She scoffed. "You're trying to tell me you'd stay in a flea bag motel?"

"Fuck no, but if that's all I have to stay in, I'd rather that than outside." He pushed the door open.

The bed was as plush as the carpet. Pillows galore, dark tones decorated his domain. She wondered if he made the bed himself, or had maids who came in. Probably maids. She couldn't see Ian arranging pillows on the bed. Neither could she see him straightening the wrinkles in the sheets and comforters and tucking in the corners.

His words made her wonder but that's not why they were here. She unzipped her skirt and let it fall to the floor. The faster she got out of her clothes, the faster she'd get over any insecurity and awkwardness about being naked in front of him.

Ian stopped at the bed and tutted. "Stop." His gaze roved up and then back down. "Come here to me."

Jocelyn's fingers fumbled over the suit jacket's buttons

at the command but she shuffled to him. He'd settled on the edge of the bed and that made him eye-level to her breasts. Ian cocked his legs open for her to slide right in. She did. His thick thighs bracketed her knees.

She wasn't close enough to feel the thick length of his erection. A shame because his cock sat up, proud and needy, pressing against the slate gray slacks in a way that made her mouth water. This close, the scent of his aftershave filled her next breath—decadent and musky.

Slowly he unbuttoned the suit jacket and shirt, pushing them open, exposing her lace-covered breasts. "Tell me, Joce, what haven't you done?"

He started at her collarbone and trailed his fingers over the rise of her breasts, over the edge of the black bra as he held her gaze.

Aroused already, she found it hard to breathe normally. "Think it's safe to say everything you probably have."

"So you need to catch up before things really get interesting between us?" He traced her nipples through the thin material with his fingertips.

She trembled and nodded. His fingertips drew smaller circles, softly flicking at the sensitive buds. Heat scorched her skin.

"Not good enough." He'd started the caress back up to her collarbone. Once at the top again, he let each finger have its turn teasing her nipples on his way down. He tugged lightly at the tips with his forefinger and thumb and then started over. Enraptured with the sensations, all she could do was shiver and let his fingers work their magic.

"I want you to *tell me*. All the things you've fantasized about. That'll be the first task to do all the things you've never done. You have to ask for them. Maybe even beg for them. Otherwise, how else will I know?"

Her breath shuddered out. He grunted. "Take off the rest of your clothes. I want you bare." He dropped his hands back down to the bed.

Nerves filled her stomach. This felt like seduction. No. More like a stripping down of all that she was. One layer at a time. Ian sucked in a breath when she'd stood in front of him without a stitch of clothes.

He held her gaze. "You're a bonnie lass, aren't you?"

He had the nerve to joke right now? She bit her lip but ended up smiling anyway. "No idea what that means, but I like the sound of it."

"You would." His voice was gruff. "Now tell me what you fantasize about. When it's just you and your hand, what makes you come?"

At his words her nipples grew taut. Jocelyn licked her lips. She knew these were the rules for what she wanted. She had to tell him or he'd show her to the door. He'd given her the chance to walk away, but half mad and horny, she followed him from the museum to his home to have this, to have him without a whit of guilt. How many times in her life would she get the opportunity or, hell, have the guts to do this? Never if she didn't do it now when nothing was on the line.

Her heartbeat shot into overdrive. "I—He's—In my fantasies he's sucking my breasts and massaging my clit. That's the first thing he does."

His gaze lit. "Not so hard to say, was it?"

"Easy for you to say." She chuckled. "You're just sitting there looking pleased."

"I am."

He splayed his hand over the hair covering her mound,

groaned low and let his thumb dip into the crease, right to the entrance of her sex. She sighed, spreading her legs wider to give him better access. He smeared her heated, liquid arousal over her clit, back and forth, making the nub swell. Using his other hand, Ian grasped her left breast, light at first until she rocked her hips into his thumb. His groan was a thing of beauty and stoked a more potent response than his hand. She didn't know what to do. Her mind had shut down any thought.

He rubbed his thumb over her in circles, catching more of her cream to ease the way around, and caressing the outer lips of her pussy with each rotation. Tilting his chin, he tucked her nipple between his lips and sucked the dark brown peak into his mouth. Her fantasies had never been this vivid. Of course, they couldn't stand up to a man's mouth and hand. He made her the center of the universe and asked for nothing in return as he sucked her nipple and rolled her clit. All because she'd told him that's what she desired, he'd do it until she came.

She couldn't have imagined the deep, abiding pleasure of telling this man suck me, fuck me and him obeying because the words had been spoken.

The heat built in small degrees, flashing over her skin, but the intensity sprang from both his mouth and hands. His tongue wet and laving over her nipple. His thumb slick and sliding over and around her clit and the inner lips of her pussy. Teasing, enticing caresses.

Her pelvis thrust forward, stilled. She lost her breath. Clenched but nothing was there to tighten around and milk. The orgasm ripped through her. She gripped his shoulders. He grunted, turning his face into her other breast but not letting go of the grip he had on the left one.

And he kept up the tortuous rhythm of his thumb. She shuddered, hard, and her nails bit into his shirt. It wouldn't surprise her to find crescent-like tears in the silk later.

Jocelyn didn't care. Her head fell back and she crooned as she came. His teeth sank deep into the skin around her nipple. It should have hurt. Instead, the sting shot straight to her core, extending the already exquisite orgasm.

She tried to catch her breath but it was way ahead of her and her racing heart. She looked down into Ian's gaze. The corner of his mouth was quirked up and he kept a slow, back and forth caress over the hooded nub that kept her shuddering, kept her pussy tingling and weeping at his touch.

Ian loosened his grasp on her breast but only to lovingly pinch the brown peak. "Are you ready to tell me the rest?"

He looked so much like a sex god, so smug at making her come without even unbuttoning his shirt. That wouldn't do at all. Not if they went at this for the next twenty-nine days as she envisioned. He couldn't have the upper hand all the time.

Jocelyn wasn't as experienced in the bedroom, but she knew enough. Men could turn into primitive beasts with the right provocation, especially in the bedroom. He hadn't stopped touching her, leaving her bare and open, so it took no courage to say, "That wasn't fucking me. I'm already disappointed."

The gray in his irises darkened, and he eased her back, stood, turned her around and pushed her onto the bed. There was nothing but a soft sea of mattress and satin that felt cool against her skin.

"Arse up," he growled.

Even with the command, Ian's touch was gentle as he glided his hands down her spine, repositioned her the way he needed—spreading her legs wider, back arched higher, and face pressed into that cool satin. A wanton thrill pumped through her blood. At the command, at him, the smell of his sheets—decadent, enough so she almost bit into them just for a taste—her senses felt alive. She felt alive.

Jocelyn stayed that way for seconds, though it felt like eons, until his index finger caressed the seam of her sex before dipping into her. He was getting her ready for him. She wanted to turn around to watch, but his teasing ministrations had her on the brink again. Now, she had something to tighten around, but still nothing to milk.

He dragged his finger from her clit to the entrance of her sex and stopped. His breath panted out. "Your arse is tight. Something else you've never done?"

She felt exposed and the words refused to spill out so she shook her head.

"Relax." His voice softened. "I won't touch you there unless you tell me it's your fantasy."

Her fingers loosened on the comforter and she nodded again. Her knees dug into the bed while her feet hung off the edge. He shifted behind her, his bare thighs brushing the backs of hers. His hand rested on her tailbone and then she felt him, his cock at her core.

The rubber of the condom didn't dim the effect of his dick swirling around her channel and hooded nub, round and round, lubricating him, preparing him for her. Her legs trembled and her hands fisted into the cover.

The anticipation was going to kill her. She could practically hear her frantic heartbeat. Ian felt thick and hot as he soaked his dick with her arousal, but then he pressed down into her and she *knew* just how hot and thick he was. He stretched her wide and deep in that first thrust. So full of him but not enough. She moaned, clenching her sex to keep him there. His next thrust was harder, and he groaned.

Not enough, her mind screamed. She needed harder, dirtier and something just shy of vulgar. Teasing words tickled the back of her throat, and she had no urge to swallow them. Where was the man who said fuck and meant it? That man got her off. That man didn't treat her like glass. And those words would give her what she needed—to feel alive, to feel like he craved her.

"That's still not fucking me."

His fingers buried in her hips and he thrust harder, deeper and faster. Over and over. The rhythmic pounding undid her. Heat flashed through her body and had her biting into the cover. That decadent scent reminded her of sandalwood, potent and somehow masculine. The scent transformed into a taste and filled her mouth. Musky. Man. Him. Her stomach tightened and she curled into the orgasm, slamming her ass back against him as she clenched hard and long around him.

He stopped and rode out the climax with her, his breath rasping out but as soon as she relaxed, he pulled her back, gliding her sex over his cock. In and out. Pounding. Pounding. Every time she came, he'd stop, revel in it and start again. Deep and hard.

Her legs didn't hang off the edge of the bed at some point. They'd screwed their way to the middle. If they kept going they might end up on the floor, on the other side. She now understood what he meant about breaking furniture kind of fucking. If the bed wasn't as sturdy, they'd have collapsed it by now. Yes, he rocked his cock into her but when Jocelyn could feel her legs, she rocked back. She lost track of time and the count of orgasms.

Finally, she whimpered, "Wait," and laid on her stomach, not able to hold herself up on her arms anymore.

"Tapping out," he murmured, but she could hear the laugh.

"No." She closed her eyes and sprawled on the bed.

Ian wrapped his arm around the bend in her right knee and pushed it up. He rested his body over hers and then bore down into her. Slowly. So achingly slow, he stroked her to yet another climax. This time he tensed, letting out a coarse groan before he shuddered behind her. All of his frame relaxed into hers, weighing her down into the mattress.

Jocelyn didn't care. Was sort of surprised she could put together any thoughts that weren't *eiadih agdiap blgft*. He dug his hands beneath her and rolled onto his back. His chest rose and fell on a fast pace. His heart labored beneath her ear, but all she could do was lay there.

"Your bun fell loose," he said.

"Hmm."

"I like your hair down."

"Hmm."

He chuckled. "Have I killed you dead?"

"Brraiiinnnsss."

"Fucking music to my ears."

It took a bit of effort but she rolled off him. He was right. She'd lost her hair band and her hair was damp, tangled and looked like only God knew what. They were both drenched in sweat. If she let it dry without rinsing off first, she'd smell dipped in sex, dipped in him. Jocelyn couldn't have been more pleased.

Ian chuckled as he did away with the condom, tying the end and tossing it in the small trashcan near the nightstand. "Already thinking about what's next?"

Her gaze slid down and her breath caught. Thick, hard and long. Again. She hadn't recovered fully. He met her shocked stare with another smirk. Oh, miles and miles of bronzed, sculpted skin. Old scars. Tanned nipples. Male perfection.

"Yes," she said, breathless.

"You're trying to kill me. I'm fragile, Joce," he said with a tired laugh. "Tomorrow?"

Greedily her eyes raked over his bronzed skin. Miles of muscles, too. Just beautiful. And she had an all access pass. Jocelyn was bound to hurt herself trying to get her fill.

"If you say so." She swallowed but her throat was Sahara dry.

Swinging her legs off the edge of the bed, she found enough of her clothes to get dressed. Her panties had disappeared to the depths of the unknown. Ian stayed quiet, but she refused to look at him. Things might be awkward enough as is.

But after slipping into her shoes, she chanced a glance back at the bed. Bare-assed and asleep. He hadn't bothered to pull the cover over himself. She narrowed her gaze. No. He wasn't pretending. Now that she'd stopped stumbling around the room with her back to him, she could hear the light snores and see his chest rising and falling. Sleep. He looked harmless. Like any man. Not at all like someone who just tipped her sexual world upside down.

She almost stepped forward to drag the cover over him,

but that was flirting with trouble. Hell, they hadn't even kissed. Standing there, watching him while she was fully clothed, Jocelyn still felt stripped bare like a part of her had devolved to grunts and yearnings. Not sure how to deal with that, she left his opulent apartment and didn't look back.

CHAPTER FOUR

Ian braced himself before stepping into Jocelyn's office the next morning. He'd mentally prepared for awkwardness, guilt or embarrassment. Numerous other emotions that would show last night had changed how they'd react to each other while at work. He feared she would change her mind.

Feeling half drugged, he'd awoken in the middle of the night, sucked in a breath and smelled their sex scent. He smelled of her—a sweet musk that seemed to have bite and still be completely feminine. A fragrance he hadn't wanted to shower off anytime soon.

A soft growl had emitted from his throat and he'd reached for the other side of the bed, expecting to find a warm, soft woman who was more than ready to be fucked again. He'd roll over and drag her beneath him for another round. Instead, he'd grasped at air. Curses filled his empty apartment because she'd gone. Troublesome, because he'd yet to eradicate the need for the taste of her

Pounding into her until his leg muscles screamed in agony hadn't been enough. Her come slicking his dick hadn't even touched the hunger. He wanted to know why she'd crept out of his apartment while he slept. He needed to see her in order to read whatever emotions flitted across her lovely face.

Apparently he wasn't going to get that answer just yet. He scowled at the empty office. Her degrees still lined the walls. There was the Christmas picture of her mum, da, sister and her wearing hideous matching Christmas sweaters. Tucked in the corner sat her water bottle reserves. Even Garfield still sat atop the file cabinet, but no forgotten cup of coffee cluttered her desk.

At 8:30 a.m. this was where he could always find her. Where in the hell was she?

"Oh, there you are." Her husky voice slid down his spine straight to his dick.

He faced her, gaze watchful. Her teeth sank into a corner of her mouth, reminding him of everything they'd done and all that they hadn't yet. She grasped a cup of coffee with one hand and the other rested on the doorjamb. She wore something frilly that complimented the spring weather, and her heels had floppy bows in the back.

None of that hardened his cock to an uncomfortable girth. Today, for the first time, the chocolate-brown strands of her hair framed her heart-shaped face. The glint in her eye told him exactly what he needed to know. She wore it that way to drive him crazy. There was something else there too, in her gaze, but he didn't know what it was. Didn't matter. Lust, he knew. And, no, he wasn't close to being done with her yet.

"Looking for me?" he asked.

"I need a rush job on the ritual ax. Security is here to set up the display."

He nodded. "Just one more thing to be done and it's all yours."

"Okay. I've got a meeting in five minutes. I'll check on

you when it's over."

"Aye." And then for the second time in twenty-four hours she was gone. His gaze narrowed at the complete lack of emotion.

"Curious creature," he murmured.

Her cool as a fan reaction to him this morning didn't jive with the woman he'd gotten to know over the past few weeks. Aloof, flippant and Jocelyn didn't exactly go hand in hand. Not even a joke was uttered. He didn't know how to respond to that and it threw him off-kilter.

Ian usually knew how to react to a woman he'd slept with who suddenly donned a new personality. *Usually* he dealt with it by not caring as long as emotions didn't start cropping up that complicated things more than they needed to be. Sex could just be sex. Many people liked it better when it was more. Not him. And, yet...he rolled his shoulders and scowled at the empty doorway.

Maybe not having sex with coworkers had left him out of practice dealing with this sort of thing. Didn't matter, because she'd worn her hair down.

For him.

*****

"Hungry?" Ian threw over his shoulder as he crossed the borrowed flat's threshold.

The jacket was the first to go, then the tie and finally, his shoes and shirt. He glanced back and caught the widening of her eyes and the nervous swallow. Ah. She hadn't really seen him naked the day before. He'd spent most of his time behind her. His mouth quirked into a smile, but he didn't miss a step and guided them to the kitchen.

"Can't eat. Not—" She cleared her throat and he

glanced at her again.

He laughed, opened the refrigerator. “And why not?”

“You would make me say it, wouldn't you?”

“I *must* know everything.”

“You're full of it,” she said.

“I am.”

He sniffed at the Chinese food and it passed the test. He grabbed a bottle of water and got her one too. Filling a cup with ice, he leaned back against the counter and ate for a moment. She'd taken off the blazer that spruced up the dress and heels. Still neatly covered, but what he could see was more than enough to tantalize him. Her nipples strained against the silk dress despite the warmth of his flat. Her reaction had everything to do with him and that satisfied him more. She must have tired of her hair getting in the way, because she'd tamed it back into a ponytail.

“Eating and then being contorted into a pretzel is not conductive to the digestive system.” She fidgeted under his intent stare.

“Ach. You're using big words on me. Take the water just in case you get thirsty.” He dug deeper into the container but there wasn't much left to wolf down. He flicked his wrist, rolling his watch face up and tried to calculate delivery service of pizza or anything. “I'm starving.”

“You've got nothing but bachelor food in there, I'm guessing.”

He motioned to the refrigerator and shook the take-out box so everything fell into one corner.

She opened the refrigerator. “How long has this pizza been in here?”

“Long enough to turn into a science project.” He

laughed at the look she gave him. "What? I've been busy at the museum. Rarely here. Matter of fact, this is the most I've spent in the flat between yesterday and right now, outside of sleeping."

"You've got eggs. Sandwich meat. Stinky cheese." She huffed. "You can make something."

"*If* I wanted to cook. This," he shook the empty carton, "didn't even need to be warmed."

She blinked at him and closed the door. He tossed the thin cardboard box in the trash, trying not to laugh. From his teen years on, his 'fridge never looked any different. Darwinism at its best. Order out or you'd have to scrounge around in the refrigerator for something that looked less likely to kill you if ingested. Not always that way. Not when his mum bothered to be around, but habits were hard to break. He wasn't a teen anymore though, and if Jocelyn would be here a lot...

Bugger those kind of thoughts. "You're disgusted with me," he murmured.

"That's a strong word." She kept fidgeting but ended up picking up the water bottle he set aside for her. "Baffled is probably closer to the truth. Hire someone to buy you groceries and to clean out your 'fridge if you don't have the time or the give-a-shit. I know you're only here a few more weeks, but I don't know." She shrugged. "I guess I'd make a home wherever that happens to be."

Pensive, he tried to suss out any ulterior meaning to her words but found none. He didn't treat the women he fucked with disrespect, but he didn't share this kind of easy intimacy with them either. She managed to bring warmth and a comfortable familiarity wherever she went.

Everything within him wanted to drive the point home

that they weren't going to be more than what they already were. Just because they'd talk outside of the bedroom didn't mean they were building a foundation of something more. Pointing it out would make him a dobber. So, he didn't, but it didn't dim the unease. *Do what you do best.* He grunted at the silent reminder, picked up the cup of ice and water bottle.

She followed him without another word. By the time they'd made it to the room, she'd scattered her clothes in his flat. He put down the water and cup on the sideboard next to the bed, unbuckled his belt, dropped out of his pants and then underwear.

"Any other fantasies you want to tell me before we get started?" he asked.

"Actually, I'm drawing a blank at the moment."

Since her gaze hadn't left his dick, he could only smile. "That's all right. I've got something in mind. Get on the bed."

"Arse up?" she said with a teasing glint in her eyes.

His dick jerked at the eager tone. "Not right now. Lay down. Relax."

She climbed on the bed and tossed off some pillows in her way. "I never understood the need for this many pillows."

"They could come in handy later."

She stilled and met his gaze. "I'm starting to think you say those things to screw with my head."

"Does it work?"

"Yes."

His only reply was to grab the cup of ice and shake a cube into his mouth. Her gaze narrowed on his face and if she had intended to relax, the action was lost the moment she tensed and sat up from the pillows. Her brown skin glowed from the sudden flush. She was beautiful and lush. He crunched down on the cube and climbed over her onto the bed. Without having to say a word, she spread her legs wider and raised her hands above her head to give him better access to all of her.

Had Joce done this before? The thought twisted in his gut and Ian had to breathe through his nose for a moment to get past the unexpected rush of jealousy. His hands fisted thinking about another man doing this with her, for her. And Jocelyn loving it. He sucked in more air around the ice, letting it cool the sudden temper.

Her breath caught. "What?"

Ian dipped his head instead of answering and outlined her areola with the ice. The effect was instantaneous. The dark-tipped nub hardened and she moaned, back arching up, thrusting her breasts closer. He cupped the soft globes and brought them together and teased her with his tongue until the heat of his mouth and her, melted the ice.

Jocelyn's thighs squeezed his and the jealousy fled. Didn't matter who came before him, she was with him like this now. She was doing these things with *him*.

The melted ice dripped down over her breasts and onto the comforter. Wet and full, her tits practically begged him to bend down and do more. He began at the curve of her left breast and licked away all the remnants of water. She whimpered, but guided his head to any place he missed. He would have smiled at her but she was touching him, moaning for him. Almost enough to do him in.

When he'd lapped all of the left over water, Ian pulled back to admire his handy work. Her nipples glistened in the soft light and every pant made them jiggle just so. Her eyelids were low, her skin flushed and she was open wide for him...Ian was on the brink of coming seeing her like that. To get his head back in the game, he reached for the cup and took in another piece of ice. Time to really undo her.

Except, Jocelyn's gaze lit with some secret thought and a seductive smile tugged at her lips. “I have a fantasy now.”

He bit down on the ice hard enough to hurt as her hand crept down her torso, lower, lower until she cupped her mound. Her knuckles brushed his cock hanging heavy between them. His teeth clenched around the cube while she petted her pussy. Pre-come dripped from the tip of his dick and moistened her hand. She moaned, stopped and ran her tongue over her knuckles to taste him then reached back down to touch herself.

All he could do was watch and try to breathe, because she started with one finger and then worked herself up to two, sliding in and over every contour of her sex. He shifted to end the torture of her hand bumping his dick whenever she pulled out far enough. Suddenly, her hand stilled and she met his gaze for a moment and then looked away.

“What?” he bit out.

She worried her lip and her breathing sped up. “In my fantasy, when I do this...he's—”

“What?” The word rasped from his throat.

“I'm sucking him,” she whispered.

Ian shut his eyes. He thought her fucking innocent and inexperienced.

“Never mind,” she added in a hurried manner when he didn't answer right away.

“Just give me a moment. You caught me off guard.”

He had to get control or her fantasy would end as soon as it started. Killing time, he adjusted the pillows around her head. She watched him, teeth leaving crescent shapes in her bottom lip. He knew what she needed and Jocelyn didn't question him as he positioned her. He sat back on his haunches at her head, straddling one of the pillows so he'd be within licking and sucking reach.

Still, he hesitated, because this was not how he imagined the night would play out. No complaints, but her shyly, whispered words kept raking over some raw part of him. It left him feeling off-kilter again and out of control. She wanted him in bed, because that's what he could provide. He would as soon as—

She didn't wait for him to make up his mind, but turned her head and licked the tip of his cock. Again, pre-come rose to the slit and they both moaned when she lapped it up. He bent forward, buried his fingers in the soft strands of her hair and held her still. Taking himself in his hand, he traced her waiting mouth, teasing her—fuck, himself—with the action.

She made a greedy sound in the back of her throat and he fed her more of his dick. Her mouth was hot and wet. He wanted to rise from his haunches just to fuck her throat, but held back because this was her fantasy. Hers to control and take as much of him as she wanted. Watching her mouth on him was more than enough to get him off, but he glanced down at her hand. Two fingers buried deep.

Fuck.

She pulled back, licked her lips and murmured, "More."

His fingers fisted in her hair and he rocked into her mouth. A steady thump pounded in his ears as she sucked him. His muscles tensed so tight they trembled. He couldn't come yet, but, shit, he needed to.

Jocelyn pulled away, shut her eyes and moaned. She stroked herself into an orgasm, took a second and brought her mouth back to Ian. She sucked more of him, moaning harder. The sound vibrated up his spine. He trembled. A few more deep sucks and once more she turned her head away, coming again.

She panted, flushed and met his gaze. "Fuck me. Fuck my mouth."

He rose, gripped his cock in one hand and fed her more. He waited to see just how much she could take. One stroke, two, a moan and she took him all. He groaned her name, unable to tear his gaze away from the erotic sight. One stroke, two and he was shuddering, both hands fisted in his hair and his cum spurted down her throat. Either he'd gone blind or had closed his eyes. His mind couldn't process anything but the sound of her muffled moans.

He pulled out of her mouth, shuddered again and had to clasp a hand around the tip of his dick because it felt like he'd come again. She sighed and met his gaze, skin flushing deeper when she did. Ian had to shut the image away because he was one arm twitch from flipping her on her stomach and fucking her into oblivion. Yes, pound into her because his dick was still rock hard.

He hadn't felt that way since he had his first taste of pussy as a teen. He could go for hours then. So, he kept his eyes closed, hand encircling the head of his cock until the urge felt less volatile. She wanted raw, animal sex, but that didn't mean he should act barbaric just to see if she loved it.

When he finally could look at her and not pounce, she wore a seductive smile. "You brought the ice and was trying for seduction," she said. "I had to balance the scales."

His fingers were still tangled in her hair. He extricated himself from the position. "I'd apologize, but fuck if I'm not grateful for the solution."

"Blame all the degrees on my wall. Made me smart."

He fell beside her on the bed and tried to slow his racing heart, but she shifted and straddled him. "What's next?"

"Jesus," he cursed. "I was trying to give you a rest for a bit."

She laughed. "Maybe later. I'm feeling insatiable."

He grinned. "Told you to eat before."

She leaned forward, her hair tickling his jaw line, and she nipped his ear. "Just did."

Ian groaned, flipped Jocelyn onto her back, scrambled for a condom and stopped fighting the urge to fuck her into oblivion.

When they were done, she thanked him and left his apartment. At least, she didn't creep out while he slept. For that much he was grateful...and bothered by that asinine emotion. Something to worry about later, because as soon as he laid back in bed after showing her out, he dropped off into a sex-induced coma.

CHAPTER FIVE

Jocelyn watched Ian take up the mannequin's leg with precision and fix the stockings. It took delicate touches to adjust the silk in just the right way for the time period. Usually, creepy work to see the dead eyes and even deader limbs, but under his tutelage, the work felt erotic somehow. All Jocelyn could see and practically feel was his hands working up her calf, one hand gripped around her thigh.

Maybe the eroticism had more to do with the dressing than undressing. Posing the display exactly as he imagined. He'd done that to her more than a few times over the past week. Face against the headboard, back curved, one leg up while the other was pointed in another direction. He was practically giving lessons from the Kama Sutra playbook.

And no matter how satisfied she felt afterward, Jocelyn wanted more, which was why she always left before she asked, probably begged, to stay for a little while longer until there was no more need.

"Bastarnt things," Ian muttered.

He had three more mannequins to go. The cursing would continue for a while and only worsen. And get more Scottish.

She smiled at him. "You can wait for Marcus to come and help you do that."

"I've no manicure to worry about. I won't be waiting

on an intern to do what I can do. What *we* can do."

She gripped the clipboard and sighed. She couldn't wipe the way he looked right before he came out of her mind—lids low, face flushed and jaw clenched. Or the way he looked right before he growled and did something totally caveman to her. Or the fact every night that week, when she looked in his refrigerator, there was fresh food. Jocelyn was doing her best not to get caught up in the stuff outside of the bed but it was damn hard not to. He was the expert, but she sure as shit couldn't ask him how to go about these things. And all of her friends had settled down and had never really done this. Not even her sister, Kimberly, who had found a nice guy and married a few years back.

There had to be a way to test the waters in order to find out how to keep fanciful longings and dumb needs under wraps. He'd made it clear it would never be more than fucking. At the time, Jocelyn hadn't thought she could want more from him. Then again, she'd believed the kind of man who'd go for this sort of fling was heartless, cold, lacking, aloof...so far from Ian who bought fresh food just for her.

She blew out a breath and then her mind caught on a thought. Taking in the mannequin and the time period they were setting up, the idea picked up speed. "How did men during this time get their jollies off without ending up married?"

He flicked a glance her way. "Carousing?"

"Hmm."

He lifted a shoulder in a shrug. "Paid for it. Picked up communicable diseases along the way while they dined on the common sins of man. Many people saw it as God's way to punish them. I'm sure there's plenty of undocumented ways they got around that. Rich men had mistresses. If he paid for her to be his, then he wouldn't have to worry about what he was bringing home after lying with her."

Sounded about right. "And the fact men have always been possessive."

His brows lifted as though conceding to her argument. "My point is humans have always found a way to have sex." He chuffed and stood, looking at his handiwork. "There you go, you troublesome lass. Had less of a headache taking off a bra for the first time. More of a reward, though."

Jocelyn laughed at the unexpected insight. "Really?"

He glanced her way and chuckled. "Aye. Now we can do the dress. The stays should be easier with the both of us cinching 'er. The interns did a fair job repainting."

Not done with the questions, she stepped lightly around the issue. "America always seemed like the dirtier, more rebellious cousin, but it could be my patriotism showing."

"Where'd you think they learned it from? Ach. Have you ever met a truly European woman? All the Puritans trekked West and left all the fun on the East."

"That's horrible," she said, but knew it, technically and historically, to be true.

The things still harped on and debated here had long since been settled in more modern countries. Maybe that's how he was able to do what he did to her, in and out of bed, and not feel a stirring of more. She didn't feel the sudden urge to marry him, but, the lines between sex and emotion felt blurred. At the end of the month, after the champagne lost all flavor from the grand opening of the exhibition, she'd miss the sex...and him.

Dammit.

“You're puzzling. What is it?”

The lie sprang to her lips with ease. “Professional curiosity. Egypt's my area of expertise. Pretty much all of the inspiration for the world's literature. How they handled sex usually ended in someone being murdered. Sometimes hordes of people.”

Tenderly, he pulled the replica dress out of the box and draped it over the model. The silk laces fluttered down and he gestured to her. “Adjust the front and I'll do the stays.”

Having done this for too many different countries, for too many years, Jocelyn helped him over-dress a woman. A fake woman, but the intent was the same. Cover her up so the man wouldn't lose his mind. Nothing attractive could be seen or else the beast that slept within the man would be unleashed. Bottle up everything that made her wonderful and human and woman.

They never talked about what they did in bed while at work, but the frustration bubbling right under the surface refused to settle down. While her fingers adjusted the bust line, her mind raced. Ian had never made a question off limits. He'd never judged her. He actively fed her curiosity.

“Ask.” He tugged the stays and without direction, she straightened out the material in the front. “Ask whatever question that has you looking like a vein might pop right out of your neck.”

Jocelyn opened and closed her mouth, and then lost her nerve. “Why is it that men historically have always been able to enjoy sex without consequences?”

“Without consequences? Makes the whole process

sound like drudgery. The better question is why should there be any? We humans enjoy it. Is it hurting anyone when you have it? Are both or all parties consenting? If so, then who gives a shite?"

Here she was starting to wrap what they were experiencing in pretty bows and flowers because it was spectacular. It had to be much more than chemistry. She wasn't foolish to think sex couldn't simply be sex, but it was naïve to think what they had was more than that.

Save face. She had to. "Never thought of it that way, but you'd think with all that was at stake, it'd be dangerous to throw caution to the wind."

"Just goes back to my premise: Humans enjoy sex. Like it even more when it has a sense of danger to it. Even married couples try to find that spark. Again and again."

That comment threw her. She took him in. "You know married couples?"

"Plenty of family experiencing dry rot in the brain." Ian smiled.

If anyone else had used the same tone, Jocelyn would have said it sounded like longing. But it was Ian. A man with rules about sex that discouraged emotional entanglements on the other person's part, never his, because sex was only sex. For him there was nothing confusing about liking the person outside the bedroom.

It all ran together in her mind and ramped up the frustration until Jocelyn reminded herself of sinful, decadent desserts. Ian fed her sweet tooth. He wasn't chicken fried steak and potatoes topped with sour cream—warm, filling and just right. No point in wanting the latter, she already had indulged on that kind of man most of her adult life.

So..."Is that your intellectual thesis?" She tried to joke with him, but wasn't sure if she pulled it off.

"Aye. Hitching yourself to one person for the rest of your life and having wee babes that look cute and gurgle. Pretty much all that babes are good for. Seems to be the only explanation is madness."

"Maybe they are. Maybe they aren't." She shrugged. "I can't judge."

"How nice of you." He didn't say it in a condescending manner but as a fact. "Unfortunately, they would be judge and jury on our lives." He grunted with feigned disgust. "Look at how sad they are. Single. Lonely. Having nothing but sex, sex, sex with no meaning to their life other than a good night's rest. Mind you, they haven't slept in eons and can't quite remember what it's like anyway."

He said it in the driest of tones. She couldn't help but laugh and the frustration lessened even more. "I have nothing against what makes other people happy."

He looked at her as though the answer was obvious. "'Cause you're nice."

"And you're not?"

He made a face. "Sixty percent of the time. The rest I'm a dobber."

He often called himself a dick. She wasn't seeing him in a kinder light because of great sex. He didn't have some deep well of emotion just lying around for her to discover, but he wasn't cruel. She knew and had experienced that first-hand. Ian was far from being a dick, but she could tell by his expression he believed it.

"You're mocking siblings," she guessed and sidestepped the minefield.

He shook his head. "Some friends who traded in their

traveling clothes for tweed jackets."

"You're the last hold out. No wonder you don't have kind words for them. Holidays they team up against you and try to hook you up with their friend or the person they came across in the grocery store who seemed so nice. A virtual stranger if that's what it takes."

He tightened the stays as he looked at her. A pensive expression darkened his face. "Worse for you, I'm guessing."

"Nothing more depressing than seeing a woman alone. Especially when everyone else is hooked up." She tried to hide it but bitterness leaked through her tone anyway.

He finished the tying, and she slapped at the dress to straighten out all of the extra folds. When she looked up, Ian's good humor had vanished. Her lungs constricted and her heart fluttered. Not in fear but of what she feared of feeling for him—way more than lust.

"*He* was a bastard." No warmth in his voice, nothing sexual, just hard words spoken.

She kept the tremble out of her voice by sheer will. "Who?"

"Whoever broke your heart."

She jerked her shoulder and let out a quiet breath. "What makes you think I didn't break his?"

He concentrated on the stays. "When it's right and good both hearts usually end up broken when the relationship is over, but since I know you and not him, he's the bastard in my book."

She ducked her head and pretended to fix the bottom of the dress over the legs.

He stilled above her. "Did I go and make you cry?"

"No," she said softly, which was the truth. She just felt

exposed. With nothing left to pretend to do, Jocelyn straightened to meet his gaze.

Except he was paying attention to the way the ties fell over the mannequin's bustle. It gave her the courage to ask, "So, who's your bastard?"

Humor glinted in his gaze when he finally looked at her. "If I told you, you'd feel sorry for me instead of understanding I was a lucky bastard. I got to love my Sadie."

Ian stopped what he was doing and pulled out his wallet. Taking out a picture, he offered it to her.

Wary, because she knew that glint, Jocelyn took it, looked and guffawed. "You're a jackass."

She slammed the picture of a *dog* into his chest. And from the belly up pose of the picture, a male dog at that.

He didn't even crack a smile. "Never underestimate the love a man has for his best friend. When I decided to travel around the world, I had to take him to the pound. No one wanted something between a Great Dane and German Shepherd."

"Sadie looks like he ate small children as a snack." She crossed her arms and eyed him. He put the picture back into his wallet and the wallet back into his pocket. "So, that makes you lucky, how?"

"I knew without a doubt he loved me." His tone was light but none of that emotion showed in his eyes. "And like I said, that makes me one lucky bastard."

She hadn't told Ian who *he* was. Ian wouldn't spill that heartache either. Maybe it had nothing to do with crossing some line between what they were because even if this wasn't just sex, Jocelyn didn't want to talk about Reese. He left her for a woman who was ready to settle down right that moment instead of in a few years. Apparently, what she believed they had wasn't all that spectacular if he didn't love her enough to wait. Or even, the life they would have had didn't make her ache in a way that waiting seemed insane.

She sighed, brushing away the memories. "Maybe I should get a dog. Never had one."

"Not even as a child?"

"Father was allergic."

He shook his head. "So sheltered. We've got to toughen you up before I go. I can't just move on knowing I'm practically leaving you to the wolves."

"I should be offended, but I agree." She went to get the shoes out of the box across the room. Hard to replicate, they had to use the originals for the display.

Tucking on the white gloves, she said, "There's no way I can go back to ordinary after this. You've made me like dirty sex too much. It's hard to find a nice guy who's also a freak."

"So, I've ruined you?"

Jocelyn didn't have to turn around to see the pleased smile. She couldn't let the egotistical comment stand. "Less you and more me, because all the stuff I've asked for were things I already fantasized about. I'll have to find someone else to do them with after you go. Teach someone else what I've learned about myself." She grinned, practically seeing his annoyed expression. "You know, since the student has surpassed the teacher."

"I can't have that then. I've got a reputation."

She stilled at the low tone and closed her eyes. His voice was husky and a little bit raw. Ian only ever talked to her like that when they were naked. Hearing him now, *like that*, at work, felt like she'd brushed up against a live wire. Within seconds her panties were damp and her mouth dry. Damn.

It was inappropriate and grounds for firing to screw at work, but it was barely ten in the morning and waiting until five felt impossible. What had she turned into letting him have her in every way, in any way she asked for? A nympho, apparently. She tried to breathe through it and didn't turn around to him just yet. If she did and he looked like he was one swallow away from devouring her, all bets were off.

She handled the antique like a good curator was supposed to and let the quiet eat away at the anticipatory tension in the air. Jocelyn counted her steps back to the mannequin and knelt in front of it. Sucking in another breath, she placed the shoes on the stiff and lifeless feet. Shoes that cost way more than when they were made.

Her skin prickled. Ian was watching her progress or just watching her. In order to get through the ordeal and keep her hands steady, she told herself it was in a professional way. Professional curiosity. He just wanted to see how someone else in their field used ingrained techniques to dress inanimate objects with priceless and irreplaceable pieces of history.

He was *not* watching her because she was practically kneeling at his feet and he liked her in that position. Her kneeling would feed his desire to see her bend on his command. Ian wouldn't get off on the feeling of authority or power, but in her supplication. Nothing drove him over the edge faster than when she gave him permission to let go and do what he wanted. The whole exploration in his bedroom was about her and he never let her forget it.

Even though she told herself not to think about it, because fanning the flames only made the heat building at her core hotter, Jocelyn's imagination snagged on how she wanted him to do things she hadn't thought of yet. She was wet, already from the flirting with the thought of him being aroused. None of this would be an issue if he'd kept that tone under lock and key while they were at work. She finished dressing the shoes on the model, braced herself and stood to face him.

Damn.

He hadn't been watching her in a professional-curiosity way. His hands were stuffed in his pockets but there was no missing the bulge in his pants. How could it even be possible that looking at a man could make a woman so wet? Being near him was enough to turn her on.

Her breathing grew unsteady. “Ian, stop looking at me like that.”

“Can't at the moment.” His lids lowered.

What he wanted to do was right there in his gaze even if she couldn't see the bulge in his pants. No. Two letters. Easily spoken, and she would mean them if her mouth could work properly. He was the expert at this but even she knew taking things out of his bedroom would blur the lines they were already crossing.

No.

Just say it.

No.

She licked her lips and he grunted, jaw clenching and Jocelyn knew what that sound, that expression meant. He wanted to take her raw and hard. No pretty words. Just grinding into her until her muscles and bones turned into liquid and all she could do was moan.

And she would love every moment of it.

He looked away and tension rippled through him. The moment reminded her of how they stood in the basement for countless hours, wanting each other, denying that desire. No thought was involved. Her foot just stepped forward, closer and the frisson between them sent goose bumps up her arm. She swallowed and let her fingers brush against his hand.

He met her gaze and something downright wolfish passed behind it right before he grabbed her hand and practically dragged her out of the room.

CHAPTER SIX

Her heart flew into her throat at the sound of Ian locking his office door. Nerves forced her to catalog every detail. The cherry wood desk had neat little stacks of office supplies, a closed laptop sat in the middle. A behemoth armless leather chair guarded a corner in the office and next to it a small table. To her surprise, decent copies of his degrees lined the wall above the file cabinets. Outside of those personal touches, there was nothing of him in the office. Just like his apartment.

She would have asked an asinine question to fill the silence, but then his hands wrapped around her waist. He pressed his lips to her neck and began to unbutton her suit jacket, then shirt.

"We're going to play the quiet game," he said and didn't sound like himself at all. He sounded gruff and half-mad, which spurred him to drag her in here with him.

She must have been too, because she said, "The first to moan loses."

Ian's fingers curled into the demi-cup as he pulled her bra down for better access. She bit back the gasp when his fingernails grazed her nipples. Heat. So much heat built inside her and her skin tingled wherever his lips touched. No way in hell would she win. With one hand he massaged her breasts, back and forth, caress, squeeze, titillate. The other hand lifted her skirt and slid into her panties.

Ian cursed. The only word he uttered before plunging his finger into her and clamping his mouth onto her neck just the way she liked it. Jocelyn lifted her arms, grabbed two handfuls of his hair and held on because this was insanity. And the moan was right there, building in her chest but she didn't make a sound. She had to remember this was a game or she just might lose it.

Suddenly, he pulled back, lifted her and dragged them to the chair. He didn't give her time to turn around to face him. They fell into it, but already Ian had bunched her skirt around her waist and spread his legs. His breathing was unsteady, a heated reminder against her neck. He loosened the hold on her waist and she turned to get a glimpse of him. Her stomach tightened with need at the sight. This wasn't the same man who always had control. A flush had risen to his cheeks and though his brows were furrowed, there was an untamed intensity about him.

Ian shifted and pulled out his wallet. There was Sadie again. After a little more rummaging, he took out a condom and placed it on the table beside them.

His gaze lifted to hers again and she expected him to smile, to soften the moment. She'd expected him to look at her with anything other than the tortured expression he wore. She held her breath, waiting for him to say something to ease the tension. This was too much for what they should be. But, he didn't. His blue-gray gaze drunk her in.

It was then she became fully aware he was dressed while her clothes were in disarray. Jocelyn shucked off her coat and shirt, but left the skirt and bra. She stood to slide out the underwear, and he ran his hands up her legs, tangling with her fingers on her legs. The simple touch started a fire deep in her chest.

He continued to help her step out of the thin satin, but kissed the bared skin along the way. His warm mouth ignited the passion further. When the silky material lay on the floor with her jacket and shirt, he kept right on kissing his way back up while he unbuckled his pants.

"Bend over," he whispered over the curve of her ass.

She did, exposing herself to his mouth and he showed his appreciation. Both hands splayed on her ass cheeks, he spread her more, and kissed her sex deeply. She bit down on her lip to keep in the moan.

Ian took his hands away and let his mouth do most of the work of bringing her to the edge. He licked and suckled her right *there* and if she breathed any harder, she'd pass out from hyperventilation. Blood rushed to her head anyway from the bent over position she was in. She felt dizzy. Her legs trembled as she tried to keep still. She didn't want to miss one lick or suck. Jocelyn had to reach back to steady herself and found his legs bare, too. When had he taken his pants off? How?

Who cared, because, oh, gawd. She was going to come and the moan she held back would leak out. "I can't," she said.

His only reply was to lick her slowly from her clit to her aching entrance. She gasped because he kept going right over the tight rim of her ass. The sensation didn't have the same intensity of his mouth on her clit, but it felt good, made her pussy clench from need. She yearned for a fantasy she'd never thought to imagine. It made her feel wanton and just shy of kinky.

She moaned.

He tore his mouth away and she moaned again this time in frustration. He grunted deeply and she looked back to see what made him stop. His hand was fisted around the head of his cock. Had he been stroking himself? Another moan escaped, because she wanted to see him do that, too.

"Ian?"

"On it," he growled in answer. He snatched up the condom, slid it on and wrenched her down on top of him. Pussy lubricated from his mouth and her arousal, she took in his cock with ease. Another moan slipped out as he spread his legs wider, spreading hers too in the process, and she sank down lower.

"We've got to be quiet or we'll be caught."

She clenched, aroused at the thought, but fear still pumped in her heart too.

"Like that, do you?" He cursed, lifted her up by the waist and slammed her back down. Again and again.

With hotly, whispered words he weaved a naughty fantasy of someone hearing them, listening and getting off. Even with that, she contained her moans and that only seemed to turn her on more. And the intensity of holding back such a simple urge gripped her, flushed her skin and tightened its hold until she shuddered from the strength of it. Ian grasped her waist and pumped faster into her. When she came, hard, he clamped down onto her neck with his teeth. The blinding pleasure drowned out any pain the bite may have caused. He shuddered too, but didn't make a sound. One clipped moan managed to get away from her.

For a while all they did was breathe heavily. Finally, she looked down and saw his pants tangled around one foot, but he still wore his shoes and dress socks. His fingers were gripped around her bunched up skirt and she'd lost a heel at some point.

A laugh bubbled up and then spilled out when Jocelyn couldn't stop it. "I wish I could have a picture of this moment."

He snorted and the release of air ruffled the hair at the nape of her neck. "Aye. Something to remember us by."

She thought about that. He had rules about having sex with coworkers. A rule didn't become one because you never tried it. "Have you ever...done this at work?"

"No," he said softly.

Her mind tried to go down all sorts of serious and relationship-like paths with him, but...he'd—they'd both been a little swept away in the moment. They'd both done something they'd never normally do with each other. Didn't mean a damn thing. She let it go. Had to.

"Well, now we have to go back to work rumpled." She laughed again, forced it out this time. "I won't be able to look you in the eye, but at least make sure I've got all my buttons straight."

Jocelyn adjusted her bra first. He placed a kiss on her shoulder blade. She stilled at the intimate touch post-sex.

"You're going to give us away with your nervous giggling." He sounded amused.

She tried to relax but couldn't. There was nowhere to run. They were at work, not his apartment. No time for a cooling off period where she could distance herself from what they'd done, and then he'd gone and kissed her shoulder.

"You started it." To her surprise none of the conflicting emotions showed in her voice. "Let this be an understanding. Do not look at me like that at work. There'll be consequences."

"But you lost the game first," he said, voice still husky. "More than once, actually. I'll be collecting my prize later."

This time the word came easier. "No. Not tonight. I've got to attack my bucket list that's outside of the bedroom."

"I have been monopolizing your time, but I will collect. Don't doubt it."

There was nothing in his tone that sounded like he cared one way or the other, which was good. The expert in this wasn't wavering. So, she'd take the cues from him. Rising, she put herself back together. By the time she faced him again, he didn't look too bad. His hair was a mess from her fingers. Since she refused to let herself touch him when it wasn't about to lead to more, she pointed it out.

A crooked smile graced his handsome face and he roughly finger combed his hair. "Next time, be gentle with me, Lass. I'm fragile."

She took the ease and ignored the discomfort. "I know. Poor Scot, getting ravished during work hours by an American."

His smile widened. "You've ruined me."

No way in hell she had, but, that, Jocelyn didn't point out.

*****

The ritual began and it was barely twenty 'til five, Ian noted. Jocelyn shook out of her suit jacket and placed it haphazardly on the floor. She checked her purse at least twice for her car keys—an item she grabbed out of her office thirty minutes before, and she had kept a good eye on the red leather. Her ordinary end-of-work ticks.

In and out her feet crept out of the shoes whenever

she stood still. She didn't stand still long in between the final follow ups with security. More than five displays were up in the show room. One hundred feet wide and long, the room was cordoned off to patrons but still a security risk for the priceless items. Not once she did waver from her professionalism throughout the day despite what had happened in his office. It seemed to Ian she held it closer than usual.

He hadn't meant to incite an incident between them. Couldn't even say what word or movement began the downward spiral of need and want for her. But the need for her made him lose his head. Screwing at work? What the hell had he been thinking? There was a guarantee of sex in the very near future, but still he couldn't wait.

He only knew something shifted inside him around the time he mentioned the married couples he knew. A collection of friends and colleagues he'd known over the years. They always welcomed him when he dropped by for a visit. It always amazed him how their lives changed so much in such a short amount of time. Most were in his field. They'd traveled. A lot. They stopped when shot between the eyes with love.

Whenever he had a bit much to drink and was feeling dreary, Ian had the occasional daft urge to follow in their footsteps. Brain swimming in drink, he'd think *maybe* after he finished breaking his neck to get the exhibition around the world, build up his rep, he could let a woman shoot him between the eyes and make him *want* the madness. An unlikely affair though, no woman ever looked at him with love.

But, aye, the need and want shifted at the mention of marriage, heightened when sadness crept into Joce's usually bright and teasing gaze. He simply didn't question the primitive awakening and blindly sought out a way to get her naked and trembling. All that with one glance from her.

Troubling, to say the least.

Jocelyn's mobile rang and she lunged for her phone in the purse. Answering it, she paced a few feet away. Only hearing one side of the conversation deepened Ian's scowl and his fingers fumbled over the buttons of the replica dress.

"I'll be there in thirty minutes..."

"Just hold on until I get there..."

"Yeah. Absolutely can't wait. So excited..."

"Well," she laughed, "I guess I'll owe you one then."

Who was she flirting with? Jocelyn hadn't said what she'd be doing after work. Not that he cared. They weren't in a relationship. Leaving faster than the speed of light after their every session was more than fine with him. But —no doubt there was a man on the end of the line. And she was excited? To fucking do what?

He continued buttoning the million useless buttons in the front of the dress. But...his mind thought of all the things they'd done. Her enthusiasm made up for any inexperience she might have had. She joked about him ruining her for all other nice men. And he'd joked back that it was he who was ruined. Somewhat the truth. He wasn't anywhere near close to being done with her.

He tried to straighten up their work area and not think about how she sounded talking on the mobile or how she'd turned her back to take the call. Ian shouldn't give a shit, but he wasn't done.

Aye, he was worried a little that he may never be done,

but nonetheless, things would end when he left. He enjoyed his affairs, but didn't linger or leave anyone waiting for him. It was unkind leaving someone waiting, hoping you'd come back. Even worse to hear through the grapevine you'd moved on.

Ian severed his affairs, not coldly, but in a finite way where there was no left over hopes he'd change his mind. He'd do it again with her. Had to. Not like she'd roll out the welcome mat and ask him to stay. He was a number on her bucket list. One he willingly volunteered for, because that's what he was good at—fucking. He'd made that clear to her from the outset of this affair. Why get mad at her now for sticking to their agreement?

He glared into the lifeless eyes of the mannequin.

Jocelyn ended the call and despite his better judgment, Ian turned around to see her face. Flushed. *Sodding bastard.* He'd already done too much by looking at her, letting her know he'd been listening. It showed he cared what she was doing instead of coming to his flat. So, he wouldn't ask.

Her teeth worried her lip as she put the mobile away. "Being impulsive is on my bucket list. Apparently."

Not a word. Not one fucking word, but he raised his brows. If she was going to continue, Ian wouldn't stop her, but he wouldn't ask.

Her feet slipped in and out of her shoes. "I'm going to see a man about a dog."

"Ah," he said and frowned. "In a literal sense?"

"Yes, checked Craigslist."

"What?" Ian said sharper than he intended.

"Adopting would take forever," she rambled on. "If I passed muster, and I really want a puppy. Now."

"And what'd you do for a sitter while at work?"

"Sister. Already called her during my lunch."

The muscles in his shoulders still felt tight. "You're going to a man's house. Alone? A stranger? Who posted pics of cute puppies?"

She sighed. "He's not a masher."

"How do you know?"

She smiled. "Saying he sounded nice and sane won't change the expression on your face, will it?"

Was the woman crazed? Was he? Ian felt like he was. "I can't let you go there by yourself. Do you even know what a dog needs?"

"Figured I'd ask the people at the store." She paused. "Are you angling for an invite, Ian?"

"No," he said without thought but then his mind started to work overtime.

Jocelyn was very much a grown woman who could make decisions on her own. Smart enough to do research and glean from that what she needed to design an exhibit and capture breathtaking moments in history. Clever enough to leave his flat before he was forced to ask her to. From what he picked up on, she had many relationships before him, but maybe only one major encounter that spurred her need for a bucket list. If the man hadn't put that haunted look in her eyes, Ian would have thanked him.

She could take care of herself, but he didn't like the idea of her meeting someone from Craigslist alone. They weren't in a relationship. They were having sex. They were coworkers. Didn't mean he'd want to see her hurt. What exactly did he have to do after work since she wasn't coming over? Nothing.

He was on her bucket list and going with her would be no different. "I'm coming."

"I should be annoyed you invited yourself." She blew out a breath and considered him without deeper meaning, but with general affection. "But I want someone to come with me now that you've made me doubt my decision about going alone."

How would he know, anyway, if she looked at him with something other than general affection? That much was good enough for him. Ian breathed easier. This wasn't a big deal. No need to give in to the niggling feeling that there was more to it.

CHAPTER SEVEN

Ian stepped into the house behind Jocelyn and caught when the interest dimmed in the man's gaze. They exchanged an imperceptible nod while she offered her hand. Taking in the home, Ian realized, it wasn't much of one.

For a man with a litter of puppies, he didn't have much furniture. There were pictures on the wall—kids but none of a wife. The children had his same fair coloring and eye shape. The boy more so than the girl, but there were no toys, no general messiness, no sounds of children. After a brief exchange of words, Ian understood why Jocelyn got the nice and sane vibe from the man—Galen probably was. He still wore a wedding ring.

Galen gestured to the back of the home, but Jocelyn's mobile rang again. "My sister. Can you give me a moment?"

"Sure. We'll be out back. Can't miss the little shed," the other man said and Ian followed him out.

"So, uh, how many places have you guys gone to look at puppies?" Galen asked.

The question insinuated they were looking as a couple. Ian started to correct the man but that would make him a dick. What difference did it make if the man knew the truth? Other than Ian felt the need to point it out.

Dobbers did things like that. Aye, he liked to mark his territory and had no qualms about it, but Jocelyn wasn't his. Still, he'd invited himself to make sure nothing happened to her. "The first place."

They stepped out under an overhang. The backyard was huge. A fairly new swing and seesaw set took up a portion and the shed took up another. He caught the pained expression on the man's face.

Ian shifted uncomfortably having witnessed the unguarded moment. "Did they pass?"

Galen blinked and shook his head. "Divorce. She took the kids. I got the dog. They can't have them where she is."

"Oh," he replied with sympathy and hoped that would end the exchange.

The man laughed and clapped him on the back. "Yeah, you're here for puppies, not a therapy session. Shall we?"

They entered the shed and Galen left the door open. The mother had sable coloring with white spots and weighed about twenty-five pounds soaking wet, but with enough bulk to not be an ankle biter. She stood and her pups started jumping up like popcorn around her. Not even fazed, she focused on her owner, wagging her tail happily.

Ian asked the proper questions as he picked up one of the pups for a closer inspection. Healthy, happy. They might grow bigger than their mum, but not by much.

"They're already vaccinated, but they'll need to be spayed and neutered. I've already done the mom." Galen's smile tightened. "No more dogs for me. Puppies are a handful."

Ian put down the dog and stood. Jocelyn's voice carried into the shed as she ended her call. He turned to her. "If you're on the fence about getting a puppy don't come in and look at 'em. They're too cute to walk away from. I'm warning you."

She halted for a moment and then closed the distance. It took a one-hundreth of a second for her to melt at the sight of them. He laughed and said to Galen, "You'll be one short by the end of the day, at least."

Surprisingly, Jocelyn asked all the same questions he had and then haggled over price with the man like a pro. Then it came down to choosing which one to take home. She started for the pup that looked just like its mum and settled on the one with white around its nose and paws. With her hands full, he made sure to get one of the blankets in the makeshift nest.

"I feel bad for taking her." She doubled checked. "Yeah, her."

Galen said, "I really appreciate it. I can't take care of all of them and they needed a home." He paused. "I know this might be asking for too much, but the kids would like to see pictures every now and again. You can just email them."

Her tone softened. "Not a problem at all. I'm a single woman. I'll be taking tons of pics."

The man looked at Ian for a split second but fingered his ring with his thumb. "Thank you, anyway. Let me see you out."

At their cars, Jocelyn turned to Ian. The new puppy cuddled into her chest, quivering and whining. He handed over the cover and she tucked the dog into it. "Now the deed is done, not sure what the hell to do next."

"She needs stuff. Lots of it, but you shouldn't take her out in public yet. Vaccinated or not."

She bit the side of her lip. "Yeah. Wonder if my sister can sit while I go."

"I can," the words left his mouth before he could consider them. Shit. What was wrong with him?

And then he thought of the possibilities and pushed the offer. "Go home and I'll bring all the stuff you need."

She pursed her lips. "I don't know."

"I've done this before. I know what needs doing."

Her gaze narrowed, because she probably caught onto his tone. "You're just trying to get into my pants."

"I am." He paused and smiled at her. "Is it working?"

"Depends on what you bring, uh..." She looked down, squinted. The pup had fallen asleep. "Killer."

"Oh, God, no. Better name."

"Paws?" She barely contained her laughter when she said it.

"Somewhat better, but you can do classy."

"Ruff?"

He made a sound full of pity. "Poor dog."

"And Sadie for a male dog was the epitome of Great Britain's and its colonies superiority over Americans?"

"It was humorous. With a 'u', by the way. You guys spell it wrong."

She grinned up at him. "Okay. Okay. Lexxie."

He eyed the slumbering dog and nodded. "I won't make fun of Lexxie then. See you in a bit."

She'd texted him directions to her address once she put down the dog. He left her behind, feeling light-hearted. He wasn't losing his mind by pushing the boundaries they'd drawn. They'd have sex at her house. To make sure of that he picked up a few extra things on his doggy run.

*****

Either puppies slept a lot or she picked an incredibly lazy one. Lexxie checked out the house and sniffed at things. If Jocelyn had been slower on the draw, Lexxie would have peed on most of the stuff she'd sniffed. But after that grand adventure, her puppy tottered around in a circle on the cover from her previous home and went to sleep. Not at all what she imagined having a dog would be like. Since she had no Frisbee, chewed up shoes or tennis balls it was kind of anti-climactic.

She didn't have time to do something really sappy like watch Lexxie sleep because Ian knocked. It hit her for the first time he'd see the inside of her apartment. Not a neat freak or a slob, the apartment was presentable. Nothing close to high scale as his, but it fit her. Should she care if he liked it?

A moot point, but nerves settled into her stomach. Before she could let them screw with her head and momentary confidence, she whipped open the door for Ian. The man had shopping bags up to his chin.

"How much crap did you get?"

"Half the store." He glanced around her apartment. "Nice place. Looks like you."

He had to push a few pillows out of the way to drop all but one bag on the green couch. The matching love seat had a huge pillow. Normally she would have sunk into the chair by now while watching TV on her flat screen, but she had stuff, so she dug in. "What do you mean it looks like me?"

"Comfy. A few surprises."

She looked up at him and around the room. The apartment looked like her office with both functional furniture and also things like pictures, replicas of famous statues only the size of her palm...little things that made her apartment a home. “Comfy?”

He stuffed one hand in his pocket and gripped the black bag in the other. “You're soft. I like it. It's a compliment. Now revel in all the doggy glory I've brought you.”

Still wary, she asked, “How much do I owe you?”

He blinked. “Pay me? Why?”

He sounded incredibly offended so she put up her hands. “It's just...not what I expected from you.”

His brows slashed down into a frown. “Well, yeah, I am a dobber.”

“Not that.” She sighed, tried again and then shook her head. “Never mind.”

Ian's gaze was intent on her face. “Say it.”

“It's just unexpected.” And made her feel for him what she definitely shouldn't. Made a little nugget of hope grow that they'd become more than sex buddies. “It's thoughtful. Thank you.” She paused, narrowed her eyes. “What's in the other bag?”

He smiled. “After you get everything together for Lexxie, I'll show you.”

Ian walked her through how to prep the food. At that point Jocelyn accepted she did get the lazy dog. Lexxie woke up the moment food hit the bowl and toddled back off to sleep once done on her new sleeping pad. It amused the hell out of Ian.

They settled on her living room floor and watched her sleep. It felt good. Not at all awkward, but she didn't know what to make of it. Was he changing the rules? Or did he do this with every woman he slept with? She opened her mouth to ask but then stopped.

Ian snorted and continued to rub the puppy's head. "That makes it twice now."

"What?"

"You chickened out on asking me a question earlier at the museum. You know history as well as I do. Yet, you're curious about mores? Ask."

Well, there was her in and no way to back out now without reaffirming her chicken status. "I've only ever been in monogamous relationships. I don't know what I'm supposed to do here, with us. Are you supposed to go with me to get a dog? Buy my dog stuff?"

He shrugged slowly. "I've made this confusing to some extent, but we're dating, in a way. It's not going anywhere. We'll end and we know that date. But, I can do things like this for you and you for me, if you want. Does that help?"

No, because no matter what he said Ian shouldn't have been there, having this quiet moment with her. Not if they'd end. She wasn't built for affairs. If that didn't make things any more conflicting, she felt safe with him. She'd asked for things she'd never had the balls to with any of her ex-boyfriends. She trusted he wouldn't think less of her, wouldn't be baffled why she wanted to explore a certain fantasy.

Three more weeks and then she'd have to find someone else who'd stay, who'd make her feel safe and trust him. She'd have to scrounge up the same courage to be this woman with a new man, but then it'd matter when they had quiet moments like this. They would be building more between them instead of coming to an abrupt end. Yes, she wanted that fantasy relationship with Ian. He didn't want a relationship, had told her from the beginning sex was all he could offer, and that knowledge dug a pit in her stomach.

Common sense told her to end them now. Get out before things got any more confusing, but he was watching her with an intent expression, seeming to hold his breath for what she'd say next. It was dumb to read anything more into the pensive look on his face.

So, she let out a breath and said, "What's in the bag, Ian?"

His mouth crooked up. "Show me to your room and I'll show you."

Didn't take long for Jocelyn to rip off her clothes and make her way to her bedroom. He followed close behind and she glanced back. He was stepping out of his underwear, bag in hand.

She climbed into her four-poster bed, onto the soft red comforter. He was right on her heels. The plastic bag rustled as he put it down and then his hands were running up her waist, over her breasts up to her hair. She trembled. The pads of his fingertips felt like silk along her skin. They were so close they were practically spooned together.

He loosened the band around her hair, leaned down to her ear and whispered, "I've a fantasy of my own."

His fingers continued moving up and down her skin. It was hard to concentrate with the pinpricks of sensuous caresses taking priority in her mind. His chest was hard and smooth at her back. "Oh," she murmured.

"Aye. Will you let me make it a reality?"

His hands had already half-convinced her to say yes to anything, but what did he have in mind? Did she care when he plucked at her nipples until they snapped back taut? His cock a hard, concrete promise pressing at her entrance...

No. Not really. She swallowed, because what did he fantasize about? What turned Ian on? "Yes."

"Lie down," he said, but she heard the smile in his voice. "Give me a moment. I'll be back." The bag rustled again when he took it off the bed. "Bathroom?"

She told him but couldn't lay back and try to relax while the faucet turned on and off, on and off. Looking at her one wouldn't know that it drove her a bit wild for Ian to spank her clit with his dick before driving into her hard. Damn. She was getting wet just thinking about it. In a sense, she knew getting her off got him off.

Seriously, what the hell was he doing in the bathroom?

The door creaked open and she laid down.

"You know, I saw you," he said, coming back into the room.

She giggled and propped herself up on an elbow. "Was hoping you wouldn't. It's killing me. What you got?"

He flipped his hand over and showed her a black piece of cloth, silk, and a...glass dildo. Her gaze flicked to his. "Oh."

"Come here." He climbed into the bed with her, resting on his haunches. She hesitated and he put down the cloth. "Nervous of what I want?"

"Curious," she said with caution.

"You can tell me to stop if you don't like it. I'm not tying you up but blindfolding you."

She bit her lip. "But you think I will? Like it?"

He made a sound of assent. She took another moment and nodded, allowing him to play out his fantasy. He folded the strip of cloth once more and pressed closer, their gazes met and she inched forward, head tilting up. His mouth was inches away and a shocking thought hit her

—they'd never kissed.

Unbelievable when she thought of all the things they'd done. On their own accord, her fingers lifted to his mouth. Not at all plump or full, but soft, paler and pinker than his tanned skin. She wanted to kiss him then to know how he tasted, if he kissed with the same fervor of passion as he fucked, but he froze at the touch.

Maybe he realized the same thing—they hadn't kissed. Or maybe he'd made sure they never did. Kissing was an intimacy they should avoid, that much she could agree with as Jocelyn looked deep into his startling blue-gray gaze. She wanted to see something other than lust. She wanted to find true intimacy, a connection in the way he gazed at her. If she saw anything, it was because she wanted to see it. Jocelyn let her hand drop away and closed her eyes.

Gently he secured the silk around her head and over her vision. When done, he pushed at her shoulder and she took the silent command to lie back.

"Relax, I'm not going to do anything we haven't done before." He added and again a laugh colored his words, "Many times."

His hand grasped her left thigh and she jolted. He made a soothing noise and slid in between her legs, one hand gliding up her torso. Maybe it had everything to do with him touching her without being able to see him do it, but her senses felt heightened. His touch always sparked an insatiable desire within her, but now it burned that need to cinders, transformed it into something new, inconceivable.

And then his mouth traced the outline of her jaw, down to her neck and lingered until she moaned. One hand continued to alternate between massaging one breast and plucking the tightened peak. His mouth replaced his hand.

The warmth of his tongue drifted from her nipples. Cold. The dildo. He caressed the tip over her nipple. The beaded nub became painfully erect at the differing sensations. He'd glide the glass over and around her nipple, spreading the moisture from his kiss, and then it was his mouth again.

She fisted her hands into the covers when he licked his way to her other breast and teased another moan from her lips with the same care. The bed shifted. Anticipation made her skin prickle and shortened her breaths. Suddenly, he cupped her mound, groaned against her skin as his fingers dipped into her wet channel. Petting her pussy, he continued the seduction on her breasts. It made her ache. Made her forget seduction wasn't what she wanted from him.

She couldn't care or think as his mouth and dildo made its way down to her sex. Slick from his fingers, he suckled her clit into his mouth and pressed the glass to the entrance of her slit. Warm and cold. Soft and hard. So goddamn wanton.

He was going to use a sex toy to get her off and she'd agreed. She couldn't see him, but he could see every inch of her. Was his cock still hard? Dripping pre-come on her comforter because this drove him over the edge? She moaned. The reality of what they were doing crashed down on her so suddenly she came without much provocation.

It didn't stop his seduction. She couldn't see it, but felt the cool glass press along her inner thigh. She gasped. He ran his tongue down to her cream and licked it all up. He groaned against her pussy and worked his way back up to her clit. Each time she came, he'd repeat the action and then work the dildo in deeper. The glass borrowed the warmth of her body. He changed the angle of thrusts and her fist balled into the comforter. His fingers brushed against her with every downward stroke, adding another element of friction that would send her over the edge, again.

He ripped his mouth away and bit into the soft part of her inner thigh. "You've drenched my hand and mouth. And I'm not done with you yet."

Words were beyond her, but she moaned her approval.

"But enough. Time for my dick to get some of that. What do you say?"

"Ian," seemed to be the only word that mattered and she murmured it. He was gone for only a moment, but really her legs and arms quivered from the intensity of what he'd done, she couldn't have moved any damn way.

He ripped off the blindfold and with no ceremony bore down into her. The toy had been nice, but this is what she'd craved. What she'd probably beg for if he made her. And she would. Jocelyn held no shame in that need.

"I want you to see you come. Watch it in yer eyes." He groaned when she clenched on his cock.

He threw her legs over his forearms and dragged her nearer. She was close already and then he began to pump hard and deeper into her, never letting his gaze waver from hers. Her moans deepened in tone and her vision seemed to darken around the edges.

"Yeah. Just like that," he said, voice husky. "Come on my dick, just like that." He reached between them and flicked his thumb over her achingly swollen clit.

That's all it took. Her pussy tightened around his thick

girth and milked him. He shuddered and thrust deeper, damn near growling when he came with her. His lips peeled back with a guttural snarl and God, she wanted to kiss him. Just run her tongue over the seam of his mouth as he made that noise.

The grip on her thighs loosened and he pulled out of her, lying down beside her and throwing an arm over her waist. He made a sound between a grunt and a curse. She held herself still so she wouldn't curl into his warmth. They were both sweaty and smelled of sex. Nothing would have been better than to shut her eyes, find the crook of his neck and pass out in it.

But that's not what they were. She glanced down at his arm. A thoughtless or possessive action? They never cuddled. They never talked about her leaving after sex. Had he wanted her to stay all those times she crept out after he went to sleep? But...his arm felt good. Her bed felt warm. She wanted to sleep too. It wasn't a big deal. If it turned out to be, they'd talk about it, finally. Or make some more ground rules. Ones that included sleeping over and how that was okay and no big damn deal.

Decided, she flopped on her stomach, pressed her face into a pillow. The movement didn't dislodge his arm, it warmed her back now. It felt so damn good. She stopped worrying about it and fell asleep.

CHAPTER EIGHT

Something cold, wet and a little rough bumped his hand and jolted him from sleep. Curved, almost whimsical bed-posts greeted his view. The mahogany wood definitely wasn't his, or the soft cotton comforter beneath his arse. Light spilled in from the hallway. Groggy, he leaned a bit to look over on the floor to see Lexxie bumping his hand, his shirt in her mouth like a chew toy.

"I really hope you didn't eat any of the shirt. It could kill you, you know?"

Glancing at his other side, Jocelyn continued to slumber. He pulled the cover over her naked form and then slipped out of her bed. Ian sighed. He was a dobber. An absolute dobber, for fucking her, for staying. For breathing in her scent and reveling in the fact that she smelled like him.

Earlier, he'd taken off the condom in the bathroom, slapped water on his face, passed by his clothes to lie down for another moment to catch his breath. He'd fallen asleep instead. She hadn't pushed him off the mattress with a nice shove if he didn't get the message to go home. Here he was, not bolting for his clothes so he could make his escape. He glanced down at the pup and scooped up the little troublemaker.

"And if you didn't swallow any bits of my shirt, you've

probably pissed on her rug. She'll kill you. It's an antique. The only one she owns from what I can see."

Gently he freed his shirt. Some tears but nothing missing. "Good, you didn't. But, I'm sure you've pissed the rug. Let's go hide the evidence."

He wasn't exactly whispering, but still Jocelyn didn't move. Ian squinted at her. Yeah. Asleep. Not faking it, hoping he'd get the message. The real question he ought to ask himself, why wasn't he gone? Lexxie whined and he pressed her closer to his chest.

He was being nice that's why. He'd let her sleep and take care of her dog while she did. Checking the time on her nightstand clock, it was barely midnight, but a long time since the last feeding and for a short stint outside.

Not bothering with the shirt, he found his pants, slipped into them and didn't fix the belt buckle. He discovered some leftover grocery bags under the sink and took Lexxie out. Done in almost a literal two shakes, he came back into the first floor flat.

Jocelyn hadn't woken up, so he prepped a bowl for the dog and wondered why he wasn't trying to leave. He meant what he said. They were dating. In a way. No need to feel discomfort for lingering in her apartment.

The sex was a bit different tonight, but of course it would be. He'd played out one of his own fantasies. No big deal that he suddenly had the urge to wake her up with a kiss and do it all over again, just as slow, nothing rough. A lingering, sensuous glide into what they loved to do with each other.

No big fucking deal if Ian wasn't rubbish a good part of the time, and he signed up to teach her to be more like him. That lingering, sensuous glide he wanted tonight only meant he hadn't gotten his fill of her yet. He started to worry he may not ever. The Kama Sutra had sixty-four positions, but that still wouldn't be enough. Some positions she might love more than others. He loved watching her love it. He'd have to do it again. Just for her.

Ach. *Fuck*.

He was leaving and there was no changing that. He'd made commitments that would solidify his consultation business. He'd be gone and couldn't ask her to wait. His father had waited for a woman. Even if his mother had only gone for a few weeks that last time, those moments until she did return would have slowly killed his father anyway. She traveled most of their relationship until one day she didn't come back. His father had been locked in a relationship with an absent partner and it sucked watching it kill a small part of his da every time his mother left.

No. Just no. Would Joce want him aside from being a good lay? All signs pointed to no and that gripped his gut hard and twisted. She'd touch his lips and looked as though she'd kiss him. They hadn't and, still, he was reeling by how much he suddenly needed to. When the woman wanted something, she'd learned to ask for it. She hadn't asked so that meant she didn't want to kiss him. He was a number on her bucket list. Exactly what he always wanted. So why was his jaw clenched so hard at the thought she didn't want to kiss him?

Lexxie whined at his feet. Ian picked her up, placed her on the island in front of him and told the troublesome thoughts to bugger off. She bumped his face with her cold, wet nose and he tried to smile. "You know, I'm half in love with you already? All you need to do is the puppy dog eyes and I'm done for."

Her butt hit the wood and her tongue lolled out, eyes getting bigger as she did. "I had to say something, didn't I?"

She did a doggy grin at him. Ach. His heart tripped and fell and Ian laughed at the light spill of emotion.

"What's so funny?" Jocelyn asked groggily.

"Lexxie's trying to wrap me around her paw and it's working."

He glanced up. Hair a bit messy from sleep, she looked confused but pleased. His stomach clenched. This was his chance to leave but his feet refused to move. Lexxie whimpered and scuttled closer to him.

"Do I look that bad?"

"You look nicely rumpled."

"No need to lie. Got a glimpse in a mirror and almost pissed myself until I realized it was me."

She'd probably expected him to be gone and hadn't bothered to clean herself up. She padded over to the refrigerator and murmured a "thank God" and started pulling stuff out.

"I'm starving so I'm about to cook," she said. "I know you're hungry. Take care of my pooch? This might take a while."

Without question, he should have shot down the invitation, but they were *dating*. He could do this. Spending time together out of bed wasn't a complete no-no. They did all the time at work. Now they'd do it here.

He told himself one lie after another until the tension in his shoulders ebbed. "Need me to move?"

She flicked a glance toward him and bit the curve of her smile. "You're fine. I know you like to watch me."

"There is that." He cupped Lexxie's bottom and

brought her up to his chest. She curled into the crook of his arm and fell asleep within seconds. "What're you making us?"

"Fried chicken, mashed potatoes, gravy, green beans and biscuits." She squinted. "Something like bread rolls, to you."

His brows rose. "That hungry?"

"Yup. When was your last homemade meal?"

He shrugged. "Haven't been home in a while."

"Not exactly what I meant, but now I'm curious. Glasgow's home, right?"

"Where I grew up. Cold for no reason most of the year, but sometimes I miss it. My brother can take care of himself and does so badly. He's a dobber, too. More so than me. And Da...he's getting older. Him I miss."

"Most parents do when you're not looking." She broke out the chicken, already thawed. She must have planned dinner earlier. A large offering for just herself.

He opened the 'fridge and looked inside. Nothing like his. Hers had order and was clean. Tupperware galore, but one could only eat leftovers for so many days before getting sick of them.

"If you're looking for the heads of the men I've slept with, they aren't in there. Grab me the flour. Bottom shelf."

"Looking at leftovers," he said and then smiled at her.

"Third shelf, red top. That should hold you over until I'm finished."

When he passed over the flour, he saw the tray of canned rolls. So that wasn't going to be homemade and that relaxed him even more. He wasn't dealing with Betty Crocker.

"Who's getting older for you?" he asked and didn't take anything out. He could wait.

"Mother. Calls me once a week with a list of things not working like they used to. Last week it was her knee. Dad's as spry as ever, probably won't retire as a principal for a while yet."

She grabbed an apron from the hook by the stove, covering the long nightshirt she'd pulled on. The tightened strings pulled the shirt up enough he could see the boxers and luscious beautiful legs. She made the male piece of clothing feminine, sexy. Already, he wanted to jump her again.

Giving the thought and her some distance, he went back to leaning against the island. There was no nervous fumbling because she had an audience. He wondered how many times she cooked for a man.

The thought lodged between his stomach and heart. Yeah, he broke a lot of ground in bed for her but not here. His gaze strayed toward the door and he sighed. No. Still couldn't force himself to go. How often would a beautiful woman, fantastic in bed, too, offered to feed him and wanted him to stay?

Not ever.

"Your mother or is it mum?" she asked.

Ah. That's why he didn't do this. "Having a great life from what I hear."

Her gaze narrowed on him for a moment, but then she continued seasoning the meat while making a noncommittal noise. "That sucks."

He waited for more poking and prodding about the relationship with his mum. Questions to see if he hated all women and suss out the reasons why he only indulged in non-committed relationships. There'd be insinuations and pity about not having a mum's love as a little boy. He waited some more but none of that came. "That's it?"

"If you wanted to spill out your sob story, you would've. Wine? I picked up some Chardonnay before I got home yesterday." She smiled at him, knowingly, and he had to smile back.

"My mum was American. She loved to travel, like me or I'm like her. Fell for my Da in Scotland. They got married. She kept on traveling between getting pregnant with me and then my brother. Eventually she kept going and never came back. Found some other man to marry and more children to have. I've heard she didn't travel as much after that."

Finally she looked him head on. "She's your bastard, and trust me, a mother who leaves her children behind without a backward glance is, at the very least, a bastard."

That had crossed his mind a time or two or three. Along with the fact he might feel different about sex, love, marriage and everything in between if his mum had stuck around long enough to keep his da, his brother and him from turning into unmitigated bachelors.

He scoffed to dislodge the bitter taste in his mouth. "Guess you could say that."

"But, the difference is you aren't leaving anyone behind when you go. That makes you a cad, but not heartless."

Warmth filled him at the words even though they were complete shite. "Is that the way you see me?"

A corner of her mouth quirked up. "I see you naked so my viewpoint may be biased."

"That may be the reason." But Ian didn't think so and he frowned at that.

She grinned at him. "Ask."

He shook his head, still puzzled by her words. "No question yet."

"When you do, know that I'll answer."

The words finally eased the tense ache in his shoulders. "You won't mind it?"

"You do it for me."

He stilled at the tone. "Any questions you have?"

She made a contemplative sound and covered the chicken in flour while the oil heated and popped softly. "More of a statement."

"And that is?"

"I know what dating is, Ian," she said but didn't look at him.

"Aye?"

"Yeah, but you're leaving, and I'm fine with that. I will be. Eat with me tonight. Leave when you damn well please. When you do go, for good, don't worry you're leaving me brokenhearted. I'm made of sterner stuff than that. You don't have to sugar-coat the ending, because the whole point of us was for me to do everything I was too scared to try."

Her words rocked him to the core. She was strong. Vibrant. Sexy. Wholesome-ish. Everything he should walk away from and give a better man a chance to enjoy. "Aye."

"You won't be *the* bastard, so relax. We've got three weeks and there are plenty of fantasies between the two of us to keep us busy."

He looked at Jocelyn, really looked at her for what felt like the first time. If he was a different man, with different heartaches and goals, he would have fallen for her right then and there. But he wasn't. He couldn't relax, not entirely, but fuck if he didn't try.

*****

Ian moved just a fraction of an inch and Lexxie adjusted her position on his right foot. He liked that. They'd played out the same scene several times in the last few days since she had first made a home with Jocelyn and still he wasn't tired of it. This time was a little different. Ian shifted against Jocelyn's kitchen island. She leaned closer to him. He liked that even more.

He wanted to see if Joce would sink her teeth into the food. She'd taken all the time in the world cutting the pork chop into fine slivers. Her lids were low, hair bunched up on one side because he'd waken her for dinner. She still looked sexy as fuck to him, lips pursed and a wary glaze to her eyes.

She lifted the fork and put it back down beside the plate. "There are no dishes in the sink. So, I don't think you really cooked this."

Ian forced his lips not to curve into a smile. "You wound me with yer suspicion."

Her gaze narrowed to slits. "You're breaking out the Scot. Now I know you're lying."

"Just taste it."

"Would you feed it to Lexxie?" she threw back.

He plucked a piece from the plate and tutted. The warmth on his foot lessened only a fraction. Jocelyn rounded to his side and watched him give Lexxie a piece of the food. The dog chopped on it twice but since the meat was tender it was gone in a flash.

"See?" he said.

She didn't move back to her side so while Lexxie warmed his foot, Jocelyn warmed his side. He hooked a finger on her plate and slid it over to them.

She looked at him and then the food. "Where'd you get it?"

He swallowed the laugh at her question. "Freezer."

"How'd you thaw it?"

"The old fashioned way of running cold water. Not hot." Something she'd taught him or, closer to the truth, something he'd picked up the last three days spending way too much time at her house.

"I don't know..." She bit her lip and picked up the white ceramic dish. A sniff and then she shrugged. "Open wide."

She lifted a piece of the pork to his mouth and he grabbed her wrist. Ian chewed the food and then licked traces of the wine and Worcestershire sauce from her fingertips. Nipping at the sensitive tip of her forefinger, he pulled back. "Delicious."

"You've told me a time or two, but what about the food?"

"Not as good as you but passable."

A dreamy mist, a mixture of pleasure and lust, clouded her eyes. Her lips formed into a soft pout and his gaze was caught in the web of the dark-pink and tender flesh. Much plumper than the lips he was familiar with but no less tantalizing. Drawing him in, teasing him because they felt off limits and nothing about them seemed to be.

Maybe a few days ago had been a fluke, and he'd read too much into her reaction. He tutted and twitched his foot. Lexxie jumped up, and Ian moved in on Jocelyn, leaning down for a kiss. Before their lips could touch, she lifted her head and offered her neck. He tensed.

Ach. No.

Letting out a frustrated breath, he straightened, grabbed the plate and handed it to her. "Eat. It's rude not to."

She hesitated, not meeting his gaze, but finally took a bite. She made a noise that sounded like a guttural hmm and ate another sliver. But she'd turned her head away when he'd tried to kiss her and Ian couldn't revel in the sounds she made. The good mood he had was slowly turning to shite the more he thought about that quick flick of her head.

Lexxie whined. He glanced down and she shuffled close to his foot again. An angry tut had her scuttling back. "What?" she asked.

The plate clanked lightly against the wood and then Jocelyn's hand, soft and usually soothing, pressed against his wrist. He threw the same question, in the same irritated tone at her.

"Are we about to argue?" she asked, voice cool.

She wanted to have a calm discussion? He felt anything but calm. "If and when we argue, it'll be loud and ugly. Don't lash out at me with a reasonable head. Arguing with heat is the only way we'll argue."

"Another rule?" Her voice was just as soothing and unaffected by his sudden temper and it grated on him. "By the way, Ian, that's some screwed logic."

Maybe, but he only had real good, high-blood-pressure-inducing arguments with people he gave a shite about. He and his brother had come to blows many of times before.

But, wait...

Why did he care about any of this? He was making sure Jocelyn was fed. He hated how Lexxie shuffled back away from him as though he'd taken a hand to her arse. He felt like pish over Jocelyn refusing to kiss him. None of it mattered, but it still felt like a stone in his gut that no amount of shifting would dislodge.

"Forget it."

She blinked and her head snapped up. "No."

"Joce," he started to speak but she shook her head.

"No." She blew out a breath. "You're right, but first I'd like to know why we'd argue, just now?"

He felt...exposed. Not necessarily with the question but the answer that immediately sprang to mind. "Like I said, forget it. I'm taking Lexxie out for a walk. I already ate, and then I'll get out of your hair."

She swallowed again and he couldn't read the emotion crossing her face. Irritation? Her boy toy was having a fit in her kitchen. How ridiculous, which is why he wanted to drop the whole conversation. But, still, he waited for her to come up with the words.

"I-we—*Ian*, I'm not a fan of kissing." She held her breath and her eyes widened.

Every muscle in his frame went tight. The lie beat at his eardrums and deep in his chest. "Aye," he spoke low.

Why they would argue or even how they'd argue didn't matter. She had just looked him in the eye and lied. She wanted to fuck him, not kiss him. Pretty clear statement with the head turn, but she was nice enough not to throw it in his face. He'd done the same with other women, rebuff them in a clear way. Too many times.

And, it pissed him off anyway. Both the lie and for caring about it. Turning his back to her, he whistled low and Lexxie shot to Jocelyn's room. Within moments, she came back with her leash clamped in her mouth. And because he did have a shite mood, he stole another small piece of meat from Jocelyn's plate and fed it to Lexxie.

Joce sighed, started to speak and stopped. She narrowed her gaze on his face and tried again. "I'd rather you be here in the morning. It's...convenient to not have to wait for the day job to be over before we can..."

She blew out a breath and looked up at him with a plead in her gaze to make what she was asking for easier to say.

He sighed too and let go of the mad. No reason for it. He should have been concerned about the sudden need to kiss her anyway. It'd pass...but then he thought about her offer, really thought about the words she wasn't saying and came to a decision. "Put on some shoes. You're going with me."

"Where?"

"To walk Lexxie and get me some more clothes from my flat. I like convenient."

Self-consciously she ran a hand over her hair. "Thank you for not saying run a weed-whacker through my hair too."

"You're messy because I made you that way. You won't mind if I mess you up again."

She grinned at him, but it didn't reach her eyes. "Give me ten minutes to look half-way decent."

"Okay," he said and tried to roll the leftover tension from his shoulders.

Her gaze caught on the movement but she didn't say a word before heading to her room. Ian glanced down at Lexxie who'd rested on her haunches, leash still in her mouth. He bent to her, the bathroom door closed behind him, and he let out a breath.

Lexxie ran up to him and began to lick at his hand. He

let her and placed a kiss on top of her smooth head. Her arse wagged harder. He patted her rump and clipped the leash on.

Scratching her chin, he gazed into her eyes. "You know I love you?"

She chuffed at him. He took it as a yes and felt somewhat better. Jocelyn came out of the bathroom looking freshly scrubbed and smiling at him. That knocked the rest of the irritation off. He'd wake up to that. Not have to worry about breaking her heart when he left. So...why in the fuck was he whining?

But the stone didn't budge an inch at the thought. It only dug in deeper when she asked him who delivered the pork. Didn't matter that he'd made it himself and cleaned up after. He told her the name of a restaurant and let it go.

CHAPTER NINE

They were practically down to the wire now on the project. They'd adjusted their speed had revved up from last minute details. Yet, Jocelyn's head was so not in the game. Forty-eight hours and Ian would leave. Yeah, he'd be back when the exhibit ended to make sure everything was packed up properly and got delivered to the next museum in one stroke. A process she wasn't necessarily needed for.

Almost three weeks ago she had talked a good talk about being fine, but she couldn't have imagined what they'd turn into during that time. For all intents and purposes, they lived together. Him with her. She looked forward to going home to Ian. In her bed. In her kitchen. In breathing distance, but since he made it his pet cause to ensure she was breathless most of the time, that was a moot distinction.

So, trying to twist the white paper and create a wig made Jocelyn a little stabby. Didn't help that her intern hovered. His last year in grad school, Marcus had a pure talent in artistry. He'd been pushing for more and she was almost ready to give him more responsibility or actually stab someone.

“Is the hot glue gun ready to go?” The mannequin's head sat on her desk. The cap had dried the day before and would be used again at some point.

Crafting the wig was the very last project and then only small and insignificant details were left. And then the opening where nothing but academics and monied folks were invited. *Then* the people she did this for. Everyday people who probably would never have the money to buy antiques or pieces of history. Didn't have the means to cross the world and see relics outside of pictures, but they could afford the admission fee. That's why she did what she did. For them.

The damn wig was standing in her way. *And* her head wasn't in the game, because Ian sat back quietly in what she called the war room watching her, pretending to work, but she knew the expression he wore. If Marcus wasn't hovering, Ian might have dragged her off to his office for a very important and private meeting.

Marcus brought over the glue gun but didn't hand it over. "I can do this. I really want to give it a try. Can I show you something?"

Curious, she pushed away the impatience and told him he could. He put the gun down and went to his area. He came back with sketches. Step by step drawings of how to put together the paper wig. Not hers, not from the Internet, but his own drawings. She could tell from the slant of the lines and the young man's personal flourishes. Impressed, she stopped twisting the paper.

The details were breathtaking and accurate. "How long did it take you?"

"Six weeks."

Half the time he'd been there and this is what he'd stepped up to do. She glanced at him, and he tried to look professional and capable, but she could see the eagerness. Although she was in charge of all the interns, this project wasn't her baby, alone at least.

Jocelyn gave the papers to Marcus and pointed at Ian. “Show Baird. He gets the final say.”

Ian sat up straighter in the chair, putting down his work on the small table next to him. He spent a much longer time over the sketches and asked for a pencil to make some small changes. Overall, he made the decision quickly. He glanced at his watch and met her gaze. Her skin prickled, because as far as he was concerned, it was time for them to leave.

“You give either one of us a call if you can't finish in time or you have any snags,” Ian said in a stern but encouraging tone he used on all the interns. “I don't need to tell you how important it is that you don't bugger this up.”

At that Jocelyn hesitated. Normally, when she didn't have a life after work, she'd have stayed with Marcus. Be the annoying boss hovering over someone else's shoulder. Hell, even when she was with Reese, she'd have stayed to gain more experience. But she was different with Ian.

In forty-eight hours he'd be gone, and unlike what she'd said in her speech a few weeks ago, she'd be heart broken. They had tonight and waiting to be with him would be insane. So she wouldn't. Couldn't.

Just in case, she wrote down her cell phone number for Marcus. She packed up her stuff, went to her car and waited to see Ian's pull up behind her. She led the way to her sister's house. An off shot from her own apartments, Kimberly lived in a home, in suburbia with her husband and kids. Her niece and nephew were home, but the husband hadn't made it yet.

Her sister, as usual, gave Ian a steely gaze when he

came in behind her, but they greeted each other in polite tones. As usual, Jocelyn ignored it. Lexxie bolted from somewhere in the back of the three bedroom home at the sound of their voices. Yeah, she tripped over her too-big paws on the way and greeted Ian first.

Her sister made a noncommittal noise and frowned at the display. "You'd think it was his dog."

"My girl's smart," Jocelyn said. "She doesn't bite the hand that feeds her."

Ian cooed to the dog as she flopped on her back for belly rubs. "There's my baby girl. How are you doing? Miss me? Aye? I know you did."

Since she knew what his hands felt like, Jocelyn didn't begrudge Lexxie for having absolutely no shame. Maybe, if Jocelyn had been on her game, she'd have realized her slip. Kimberly grabbed her arm and dragged her away from the shameless display. Her kids waved hi but didn't stop playing the video game.

"He feeds her as in he lives with you?"

There was no real way to talk herself out of this one, but she tried. "He visits. A lot."

Her sister glared. "More than a toothbrush and a change of underwear kind of visit?"

After their almost argument, he'd picked up some extra clothes. After the fourth night in a row, she told him it'd be *convenient* for him to bring all his grooming essentials too so he wouldn't smell like girl soap and look like he hadn't shaved in a year. He'd done it without comment or looking at her in a way that said they were crossing a line, which they totally were. Her speech wasn't that good, but Jocelyn refused to read more into his motives.

Sooner or later, she'd have to answer her sister, now, or

when she walked around looking butt hurt after he left. “Closet and drawer space. I cook. He cleans.”

They looked alike, so, it was unsettling to see a gaze so much like hers staring back with the same doom-is-looming-on-the-horizon emotions swirling in the brown irises.

“I know,” Jocelyn murmured. “But I wanted this, even knowing damn well how it would end.”

Kimberly sighed. “Are you sure?”

“Yes.”

Her sister turned that gaze on Ian who had straightened and was watching the game Cecelia and Lamar were playing. Lexxie took her time trotting over to Jocelyn. She bent down and gave Lexxie the same love Ian had. There was no contest. Lexxie didn't revel in it, but treated Jocelyn's petting as a chore. She chuckled and straightened, ending the charade.

“Call me,” her sister whispered. “Any time. For anything.”

“Okay. I'll be fine. Swear.”

Kimberly rolled her eyes and shooed them all out of the door. Once home, Jocelyn took Lexxie out for her daily sniff, pee and poop around the neighborhood. Didn't take long because her dog didn't meander. She wasn't lazy in that regard, at least. Back inside the apartment they found Ian had stripped down. He'd put on sweats and a Cambridge t-shirt.

He frowned into the refrigerator and then aimed that expression at her feet. “You haven't taken off your shoes yet. What's wrong?”

“I'm worried. A litany of things, but the top of the list is Marcus. I shouldn't have left.”

His gaze narrowed and he made a noncommittal noise. She laughed. He knew it wasn't the whole truth but he was going to let her have it. "It's the top thing I want to talk about," she said. "Fair?"

"Fair." He closed the door and had a water bottle in hand. "I've seen his work and you working with him. I think he's ready. Don't worry about it. It'll be fine." He paused. "Of course, he can always make us look like jackasses for trusting him, but that'll be on me, not you."

"Maybe," she muttered.

Lexxie left her side to sniff around Ian's feet. Finally, she just plopped down on his right foot. Sadly, she and her dog had it bad for the man. She wondered how Lexxie would react once she realized that Jocelyn was it, the real and only owner.

But that's not why they were home. "Season the steaks, then meet me in the bedroom. We've got some very important things to talk about before you go."

He raised a brow. "You're going to let me use salt unsupervised?"

She hissed and thought about that for a moment. "Use the All Seasoning."

"Your trust in me is breathtaking at times." He grinned at her and tutted at Lexxie. The dog rose on command, tail wagging and smiling at him with a stupid I'm-so-in-love grin.

Jocelyn sighed. *Yeah.* She kicked off her shoes, the jacket came off next and she was naked by the time she curled under the covers. Lexxie preceded Ian, but mainly to settle down right at the threshold. Her girl knew the routine, too. Ian passed her by and closed the door in the dog's face. A short whine to make her opinion known but no scratching followed the action.

"Your dog likes to listen," Ian said.

"She's a pervert like her owner. It's why she puts up with me, I think."

He tugged off his shirt and displayed the chiseled chest Jocelyn never got tired of seeing. "Oh, so you've accepted this new side of yourself?" he asked.

"Around the time you got me off with my showerhead." She tried to remember and couldn't. "When was that?"

"Yesterday."

"Yeah. Then."

He tossed his sweats at her and she caught them, pressing her nose into the soft cotton just to smell his decadent musk mixed with her laundry soap. Completely pervy, but that's why he'd tossed them at her—he wanted to watch her do it, so, she didn't feel alone.

Ian waylaid his path to the bed to break out the oil and a handful of condoms, placing both in easy reach on the nightstand. Finally he slipped in beside her, sighed and pulled her on top of him. Where he was hard, she was soft and their bodies curved together perfectly. She arched up, letting her hands sink into the mattress, one on each side of his torso.

"Feels like I haven't touched you all day," he murmured before kissing her collarbone. His hair had grown out again, curling around his ears and looking unkempt.

"We haven't if you discount the morning." She tried to say it lightly, to continue the act of not caring that this might be the last time he'd touch her like this.

Her throat clogged with all the emotions she'd tried to hide over the last few weeks. The moment his body lay warm and hard beneath hers. Or, maybe the moment her dog plopped on his foot, unabashedly needing to touch him, any part of him. Jocelyn completely understood the need to feel the warmth of his skin.

"Joce," he whispered but pulled back. "Look at me."

God, she was going to cry and then that would make it clear her speech had been bullshit from the go. It would prove that those twenty-nine years of being timid and sweetish, his word, and un-adventurous was who she really was. No, she hadn't calcified to that woman who didn't take chances—she *was* that woman already. Pretending to be someone different for a month didn't change who she really was.

She'd only proved without any doubt she was a meat and potatoes kind of woman. Ian would have every right to walk away now instead of in two days and feel like shit for doing it. She'd broken the one rule they really had. Fuck. Her eyes stung, and she tried to blink fast, keeping her face averted from his.

"Look. At. Me. Don't hide." His burr deepened. "I know I shouldn't be here. With you. Like this. So just fucking look at me."

She did and couldn't read his expression, but his head was tilted up, meeting her gaze head on. She grasped again for lighthearted. "Now all you need is a kilt."

He didn't smile. "Don't cry over me. I'm not worth it."

"I'm not. I wasn't."

She put her hand over his mouth to make him shut up. His words were absolute drivel. There was much to be said about knowing who you were, what you were capable of, accepting yourself, flaws and all. He couldn't see that a lesser man, a shit of a man, would have led her on. Made her believe they could have happily ever after when the time became right...and then leave her. He'd told her this is what they would be and nothing more. He'd stated their end date.

Jocelyn had wanted to believe that she'd be a different kind of woman, but she wasn't. That wasn't his fault. "No."

He closed his eyes and rested his head deeper into the pillow. She frowned because he suddenly looked so exhausted.

"I should go," he murmured.

"But you won't."

His lips curved into a smile and he laughed. "But I won't."

"Tomorrow."

"Yes," he gritted out and opened his eyes.

"You've got oil and that means a massage. Maybe we should do that instead of talking." She shifted, spreading her legs. He was hard as a rock, but he wanted to talk. Stubborn man.

His breath huffed out and his jaw clenched. "Wait."

She shook her head. "Done talking."

He let out an exasperated sigh. "You drive me nuts."

She smiled. "Usually because I'm always sitting on them."

"Joce," he said again but groaned as she slid up.

"You were saying?"

"We're not done with this."

She said, "Yes. We. Are."

His lids were low, voice raspy and his hands were already working their way up her spine. She teased him some more, using a fake Scottish burr. "Ach. A man's heart is not in his stomach, Lass."

He smiled and she ran her fingers over his lips. "What fantasy haven't we explored yet?" he asked.

Kissing him. A fairly new fantasy, but it ran rampant in her mind. He'd tried twice, but both times she'd dodged his lips. He'd gotten the message and hadn't tried again. Smart man.

Tonight, kissing him would undo her, so, she nipped at his ear lobe. He held his breath and she pressed closer to feel his heartbeat pound against her breasts. "You."

His chuckle rumbled low in his chest. "You've had me plenty of times."

"Never fails to get me off."

He reached for the oil and lathered up his hands behind her back. Ian started at her neck and massaged his way down and up. He kneaded out any tense muscles. The more he touched her, the wetter she became, the heavier her breathing. It was seduction, but she'd long since stopped pointing it out and asking for anything else. If for just a time she could have intimacy with him, she'd revel in every one of them he showed her.

"Sit up," he said.

When she did, he straightened and placed his back against the headboard. Face to face, he continued to knead her muscles, but now, with her legs spread open by his, he brushed his fingertips over the lips of her pussy from behind.

She buried her face in the crook of his neck and let him tease her. This was his fantasy, just touching her, and it was something he'd done often, but it never felt old. He poured on more oil and it slid down between her butt cheeks. She stilled at the thought and kissed his neck.

He tensed, hands paused. "What?"

"I have a fantasy now."

"Tell me. In detail."

She smiled against his neck and had no trouble this time speaking it, "I'm astride you like this. Riding you, slowly, and you're touching me where no man has ever touched me."

Ian's heart jumped into his throat and he cursed, because he knew exactly what she was asking for. "You've got to warn me when you ask for things like that. You know I'm fragile. Give me a moment."

But his hand was already moving down her back, following the line of oil. He heard her sharp intake of breath. She stilled, bracing herself and that wouldn't do. He grasped her hips and lifted her away from his dick. "Put the condom on."

Her fingers were hurried and clumsy, but she got the job done. He eased her down onto him, but let her set the pace. It was hard to let her go at it without his help, but she needed to feel in control of this moment more than he needed to control it. But that was something he never really felt with her. He met her strokes with light upward thrusts.

She gripped his shoulders and moaned into his neck. When he felt her tightening around him, he gripped her hips and held her still, not letting her come, suspending her in that heady moment of release. Her breath shuddered out and she trembled. Her nails dug into his skin and he embraced the pain. He welcomed the marks she'd leave behind.

Ian let her go and she rose up and down faster as though he'd change his mind and stop her again. As she did, he slid his finger between her arse cheeks and stopped at her anus. In concentric circles he prepared the tight star, felt her spasm from the orgasm. The tenure of her moans heightened.

"Bear down," he whispered. "Slowly, so it won't hurt as much."

She did and was so tight he barely breached her. Jocelyn's breath panted out and her fingernails dug deeper. She trembled, but said into his ear, "More."

He pulled out, catching more oil on the tip of his finger. He slid farther into the tight embrace. Ian had to see her face. With his other hand, he gripped her hair and pulled her back to watch. Her face looked like she was in agony. He started to remove his finger, but stopped at her soft moan.

"No. Feels good." She stroked down, pushing him deeper. A soft cry spilled out and tangled with a laugh. "Feels pervy."

"And I know how much you like that."

She bit her lip and it contained the smile. Her lips looked fuller, plusher. Ian shouldn't do what he had the mind to do but couldn't tear his gaze away. Not while her skin was flushed. She shifted, not breaking the gaze either and buried him deeper, moaning softer. He kept watching her mouth as she fucked him, fucked his finger. Watched as she loved it.

When had he gone and lost his head? Did it matter? Since he'd lost control long ago, Ian dipped his head and nipped at her parted bottom lip. She gasped and stilled because he'd crossed the line. This was something she'd never asked for and had made perfectly clear she didn't want...but she was snug and warm all around him.

Bugger that.

Ian didn't have an excuse. He wanted to. He needed to know what it felt like to kiss her before they ended. This had always been about her and he'd given everything. He felt raw and exposed for needing to kiss her, for taking her mouth without permission. He couldn't lift his gaze to meet hers. Not yet.

Her teeth scraped over where he'd bit her. "No," she said.

"Yes," he argued.

Jocelyn didn't turn her head away like she'd done before. She swallowed and sank down and then rose up again. "This."

"No," he murmured and stole another bite of her lips.

Harder, slower he sucked on the flesh as he pulled back. She tasted sweet and *right.* She tasted like perfection. Something that just settled between his throat and chest. So he had to take another taste, swirling his tongue into her mouth as she gasped and shuddered. He was buried deep inside her. It wasn't enough.

"Ask," she moaned.

His heartbeat thudded in his ears. She understood this was his fantasy. "Can I kiss you?"

She let go of his shoulders and ran her hands through his hair and gripped him hard. "Yes."

This time with her permission, he kissed her with all that he had. In all the ways he'd imagined. In all the ways that mattered but shouldn't have. She'd told him he wouldn't be her bastard. How her words made him ache.

Only a sick fuck would wish that she'd miss him, that she'd feel the loss of him, because in that moment he'd knew he'd miss her, feel the loss of her. It would kill him a little every time she crossed his mind. He couldn't bear never knowing what her mouth felt like beneath his. To feel her part her lips and give him the taste of one fantasy he didn't dare speak—her complete supplication, her trust, her heart. Wanting it made him a fool, but he couldn't not want it.

Ian dipped his tongue in deeper, exploring every inch of her mouth in between sucking her lips as she continued to take him, achingly slow. His finger worked her at the same pace, deeper until there was no more to give, gliding in and out.

She pulled back only to say "more" and kissed him again.

He groaned and slicked two fingers in the crease of her arse and down again into her, tentatively, and she lowered onto him, taking him with only a moan. He kissed her softly, slowly, hard and fast. As many ways he could as she took all of him.

He felt her tremors when she was on the brink of coming. Joce held herself still until the urge passed and then started to build herself back up. He didn't know how long they went at it just like that. It felt like forever, and if he could have, Ian would have kept right on going. She felt too good. Her moans were almost enough to do him in. And she was tight and wet. Her mouth sweet and hot.

He took her harder, rougher and she egged on him between kisses: telling him in graphic detail how it felt to be filled with him, what they could do with the glass dildo next time and how she never wanted him to stop kissing her. It was too much to hold back for either of them, because the moment he groaned deep in his throat, she clenched around him. Her soft cry did him in completely.

There was no slamming into her, only his release and hers. She went limp on top of him and for her sake, he fought the sudden exhaustion.

He pulled out of her, but kept her close. She lifted her head, glanced at the clock and then down at him, a wicked smile lighting up her face. "It's midnight. I think what we just did can be defined as a bang."

Ian snorted. "Happy thirtieth. To me, I think though. Feels like I just lost some years with that one." The smile faded, because he could see the quiet anguish grooving the lines around her. "What?" he asked, gut clenching.

"You kissed me."

He swallowed. "Aye."

Her gaze fixated on his mouth a moment. He couldn't read all the emotions flitting across her face. He only knew the one—lust.

"You're good at it," she said simply. "Kiss me again?"

Ach and he did, while her mobile rang and Lexxie whined at the door. Nothing else in that moment mattered because she'd asked and as always he answered.

CHAPTER TEN

After ten minutes and the third time her phone rang, dread filled Jocelyn's stomach. The real world had started to shatter her fantasy even though she'd tried to ignore it. Facing reality would mean ending this moment, ending them and accepting that they were never a *them*.

So, Jocelyn fixated on what she could face. Marcus was calling her. She should have stayed at work and watched him like a hawk. No. She'd tossed all responsibility for a man who was going to leave her. A man who kissed her when she'd made it clear that was the final, absolute line and that one they would not cross. She'd needed it for self-preservation and now she couldn't stop kissing him. Couldn't stop wanting him to hear what she couldn't possibly say.

No. No. Not what to fixate on. Get dressed. Go.

She pulled away from the embrace, crawled out of the bed, feeling old and creaky, and walked to the dresser. She plucked out the first thing in sight. His sweats. She stuffed them back in and found jeans, one of her shirts and trudged to the closet for tennis shoes.

"What are you doing?" he asked.

She didn't look at him. "Getting dressed. Answering my phone and then heading to the museum because I'm sure that's Marcus letting me know he's screwed something up.

Then I'll have to fix it in time for the opening. I've got a lot riding on this. Hell, we both do."

He was silent for a very long time. She knew that silence and knew what he'd say before he opened his mouth. He'd remind her they always had an end date. Her feelings wouldn't change what they could never be. Once again, her love wasn't enough. He'd taught her how to shut off emotions so she took his lesson to heart.

"Just don't." She finally faced him. "Are you coming with me or staying here?"

There wasn't a single emotion on his face but his lips were pursed. "That's it? That's all you've got to say right now?"

No time to shower. She smelled of him, smelled of their sex. Since that very first time they had...*fucked,* Jocelyn had felt he was stripping her down to her barest and most basic of needs. Civilization felt ripped out of her very core. She'd always know the things she'd liked in bed, the things she'd like done to her. Never, ever would she be able to forget how primitive sex could be. How it meant to be laid open and willing to be taken. And that made her feel like an exposed nerve.

Yeah, she asked for it, but he had to know who she really was. It would have been paternalistic as hell to pat her on the head and send her away, but he was the expert when they first started this kind of exchange. He had to know what sex like this would do to her on a cellular level. He had it all the time. Across countries. He was going to leave her exposed and raw.

Now he wanted to talk and be civilized about the whole thing? What a bastard. Maybe it was unfair and irrational to be so angry at him, but she was tired of being nice, sweet and charitable in her own thoughts. "Nothing else to say." She sounded so removed from the situation. Not one emotion leaked out. There was too many and she was just numb.

"You're leaving," she said. "For all intents and purposes, we're done. The curtains are closing. Us kissing was taking the final bow. I'm trying not to make a big deal out of this. Don't *you* dare do it."

Her phone rang again and she made a sound of frustration. "I really should get that."

His gaze stayed narrowed. Ian crossed his arms behind his head and leaned against the headboard. "No one's stopping you."

"I was waiting to see if you were coming. I'm taking that as a no."

"You've got this covered. I'm going to bed. I'll deal with the headache in the morning. Are you sure it's Marcus calling?"

Her phone rang again. "No one, not even an egotistical grad student would call like this to say 'look how awesome I am.' I should have known better than to leave him alone."

"You live and you learn, Lass, and sometimes you've got to accept some things will never change."

It took her a full fifteen seconds to hear what he'd said. Oh, Ian was pissed. His accent had eclipsed most of the words, but he looked cool as a fucking fan *in her bed*. Why? Maybe he saw the cracks and that meant she'd broken the rule. Probably turn into a headache down the line for him. God, she wouldn't make a fool of herself over him. Maybe he had a prepared speech that would soothe feathers, but make it clear they were over and she was screwing up that last hooray. She would not stand there and get those words shoved down her throat.

Her phone rang again and since she'd started this, Jocelyn turned away. She was keeping up the appearance of being just fine, fine, *fine* with him leaving. No cause for dramatics. Or tears. Just shut off whatever emotion bubbled up her throat doing its damnedest to choke her. She needed something to focus on or it would all come rushing out, drowning them both.

Still, he'd leave.

If this was real and because it was them, they'd fight about him leaving. The argument would be as volatile as their sex. Another one of his rules. He wouldn't have to tell her to ask all the questions she burned to know. She'd chuck them at him, one at a time or all at once. He'd answer them even though it might feel like breaking her, because they both knew omissions left doubts. Ones that didn't show up for some time, but they did. Reese had done that to her. Ian's mother had done that to him. They didn't do that to each other for those reasons.

What did it matter? He was leaving. No need to fight or ask questions or say things that were right there on the tip of her tongue.

So, she swallowed down every single emotion and the words felt like a handful of broken glass. "All right. See you in the morning."

"Aye." The way he said it could have shattered a diamond with one blow.

She escaped to the living room, dug around in her purse and answered the phone. "Jocelyn Pearson."

"This is Marcus. I'm sorry for calling so late, but, uh, I need some help."

"I assumed as much the third time my phone rang in a row."

"Oh, yeah. I was sure you were asleep, but I really need you to come to the museum. I don't know what happened. It was, uh...are you on your way?"

"Dressed. Have my car keys in hand. After I get off the phone with you, I'll call security to let them know I'm on my way. Don't worry about it. This is a big project even for me."

He sighed with relief. "I'll make another pot of coffee."

She forced herself to smile so it would show in her voice. "Maybe you shouldn't have anymore, but thank you for making me some."

Jocelyn ended the call and heard Ian in the hallway, then the bathroom door closed. Lexxie perked up from her spot on her bed. She looked down the hall, let her gaze rove back to Jocelyn for a long moment and then sniffed.

"Don't you dare look at me like that."

Lexxie stood, turned around and put her back to Jocelyn.

She sighed. "Yeah, I know."

She bit her lip and glanced down the hallway toward the bathroom. But what would be the point of trying to...do anything? She hadn't lied. They were done. Her phone rang. It was security. Apparently, Marcus was too anxious for her to call them. She sighed again and left the apartment. Already things felt back to normal. Work took priority because there was nothing else to look forward to.

*****

The hot water washed over Ian and he tried, really hard, to stay pissed at Joce. He knew every word she hadn't said, refused to speak because she was too nice. They'd been right there on her fucking face as she'd pulled back and realized the phone would have to be answered. Whatever had happened in bed had come to an end. They were done. And...he wasn't worth the trouble of saying another word to, of fighting with, of asking him to stay, making a mess of what they said they'd be.

"*Just don't,*" she'd said when she saw he was going to make a mess of things. *Nothing else to say.* She'd looked pissed because he was trying to turn the experience into more and not end it like he'd said.

He couldn't blame her for any of the shitty thoughts about him that crossed her mind and flicked across her face. Thought them of himself often enough. She'd offered and he took like a rutting pig. He was nothing more than a good fuck anyway. Even when there were plenty of times he felt like more with her. So, he had lived the lie because he could wake up, roll over and drag her under him. He could smell her sex whenever he felt like it. He could have her and be with her.

Ian rammed his fist against the tile and the pain sang up his arm, but he deserved worse. No. He deserved nothing. No fanfare. Just like she gave him.

"Nothing but a sodding arse."

When he told her about his mum, he should have left then. He didn't do sweet and inexperienced. He didn't do women who would make him feel... just feel. They got under your skin. No matter how long he stayed in the shower and scrubbed there she'd be. He was the good lay she had before turning thirty. He made sure from the beginning that's all he'd be.

And she was right. What could be said? *If, a big if, you do care for me, I've got commitments. You'll have long, lonely nights and not a damn thing you can do about that. You'll miss me like shit.* Even if that didn't bother her, Jocelyn didn't need or want a man with mum issues. Ach. Someone who'd finger her arse and kiss her like that was romantic.

What a piece of shite.

A whine came from the door followed by scratches. Ian closed his eyes, hands balled against the tile and gave himself a moment to pull himself together. Took a long while to stuff all the emotion and disgust away. It was years worth if he thought hard about it. Never had he felt shame for the man he was. He liked what he liked. Lived by the barest of means. What more could he want? But she made him want stupid things like tweed jackets just to make her laugh.

Fucking Joce.

Didn't she know, couldn't she see he lived with the bare minimum *to be able to* live that way? No. Ach. Fattening him up with home cooked meals. Now, most pizzas would taste like the cardboard they were. She should have turned her head when he kissed her. Just jumped off his dick and left him cold to drive the point home. No. She'd kissed him back and then asked for more to appease him, telling him he was good at it.

Worthless, useless, sentimental pish. That was everything she needed and was used to, but she'd scraped the bottom of the barrel with him. He tried harder to scoff and sneer at it, but that would mean sneering and scoffing at Joce. Nothing about her was worthless and useless. Not even her asinine questions to force him to talk, push him to be more of a man.

Lexxie whined louder at the door. Ian cursed in as many imaginative ways he could think of and slapped off the water. He ripped a towel off the rack. Fluffy but well-worn, comfy. Not at all like he was used to.

Fucking Joce.

He yanked the door open, brimming with anger, not sure if it was more at himself or at Jocelyn, and Lexxie looked up him, eyes wide and sad. "Don't look at me like that."

Her ears lowered and she shrank back. He blew out a frustrated breath and softened his tone. "Are you hungry? Do you need?"

She shuffled forward, looked up at him and plopped on his foot. He sighed. "What the fuck are you going to do when I'm not here? 'Cause I won't be. I'm leaving."

She shifted, covering his foot up to the ankle so the only way he could move was to push her off, which they both knew he wouldn't do.

He said the only thing that would get her to move, "Food."

Lexxie popped up and toddled to the kitchen. He went to the room and got dressed, took his time too because a dog wasn't going to rule him. A ball of fur wouldn't make him softer in the heart than he already was. But, when Ian went to the kitchen to get himself something to drink and eat, she was there.

He stopped and glared at her. She grinned back, wagging her tail at him. She, at least, waited until he got himself something to eat before sprawling on his foot again.

"Fucking Lexxie," he muttered and ate standing up at the island with a dog on his foot.

CHAPTER ELEVEN

Jocelyn's boss, ecstatic with the impeccable exhibitions, didn't blink an eye when she asked for a week off. She came home that first afternoon after her and Ian's second non-argument and found a note. He'd dropped Lexxie off at her sister's. Nothing more to the note.

She'd expected him back before the opening to change his clothes, but he didn't come to her apartment. She caught glimpses of him later that night, but not once did he go out of his way to say something. She could—no, she couldn't have said or done anything to change their end date. Again, she'd expected him to pick up his stuff before leaving town. He hadn't.

But really what did she think would happen? He'd apologize for giving her a fair warning? A warning he gave more than once. They had a great ride. The end. Awkward moment filled with silence and unspoken needs and then he'd leave?

She wouldn't have minded if he just rolled through for a little while to have some of her birthday cake. The one she'd baked after reading the shitty note. No. He'd left, just like he said he would

And...okay. The bastard could have said goodbye, awkward or not. Cleared out his clothes so she could pretend the whole thing had been one of those wild dreams you wake up from and sort of wished happened. Like the shopping spree dream.

Nope. She ended up taking the cake to her sister's. Her niece and nephew ate most of it. Even when Jocelyn tucked herself into bed in the middle of the night, she couldn't get comfortable without a warm, decadent musky-scented man beside her. When Lexxie had toddled into the room, Jocelyn scooped up her dog and cuddled her close.

One day stretched into the next. There were only so many times she could play with Lexxie before her dog wore an enough-of-this-shit look. The pup seemed to be just as despondent, anyway.

Lexxie would perk up at every noise in the apartment's hallway. When no one knocked on the door, she'd melt back on her doggie pillow. Her puppy wasn't sick because she continued to eat her weight in food. No. She missed Ian.

And every time Lexxie would perk up at a noise, so would Jocelyn. They were locked in their own misery. Her dog would flop down and Jocelyn would scold herself for even thinking he'd come back. The truth, she hadn't been calcifying before Ian came into her life. What it took for flesh to turn into stone was a painful process. She'd researched it.

Slowly but surely everything that felt like every ounce of *living* she'd experienced the past thirty days, really the past two months, dried up. Hardened. That was calcifying and painful as shit, and only day two.

Very early the third morning, she reached for clothes and pulled out Ian's Cambridge shirt. She wasn't going to be picky. So, she put it on and went to her sister's house.

Kimberly opened the door, one eye squinted. "Wow. You don't wear depression well, do you?"

She tugged at Ian's Cambridge shirt. The ratty sweats and tennis shoes were hers. "I brushed my hair and teeth."

"Eh. You were always finicky about that even as a little kid."

Jocelyn huffed. "And I never had a cavity. How are the wooden dentures?"

"Oh, we've reached bitchy. Come in. I need coffee."

Her niece and nephew waved. They stopped getting ready for school long enough to cover Lexxie in nothing but love. What was she? Chopped liver?

Kimberly cinched the robe tighter and led them to the kitchen. As usual the house was a bit messy but nowhere near filthy. She slumped into the closest chair and waited for her sister to stop muttering and slamming things around to make the coffee. Kimberly brought two cups to the table, held up her hand before Jocelyn started to talk. After three sips, her sister rolled her hand as though to say go for it.

"He left," Jocelyn said.

"You knew he would."

"I know."

Kimberly inspected the shirt. "He left his clothes, too. Shitty of him."

"I *know*." Her voice tried to crack, but she held it in. Barely.

Kimberly waited and then said, "When are you going to stop wearing them and throw them out?"

"Don't know."

Her sister made a noncommittal noise, eyes closed as she sipped some more. "So, you're walking around like

Raggedy Ann and he didn't care enough to take his clothes when he left. Why?"

"Don't know."

Kimberly opened her eyes long enough to shoot a steely glare in Jocelyn's direction. "Don't make me say it for you."

Jocelyn sighed, tried to say the words and chickened out. "I cared for him."

Her sister coughed and it sounded like "bullshit" before taking another sip of coffee. "You cared. Fine. I met someone the other day who I think would help you get over Ian. School teacher. Really nice guy."

It was possible that a guy—likely her niece or nephew's teacher—who read *Goodnight Moon* during the day could be into having sex in a semi-public place. He'd have that kind of adventurous sex because it revved Jocelyn's engine.

Her sister's husband was an engineer and from the way her sister lit up when the man came within breathing distance, he was probably a little dirty. Spice. Something Ian had said even married couples needed.

Ian.

Ugh. She laid her head on the table. Her sister patted her on the shoulder.

"You could call him," Kimberly said.

"I can't."

"You can. If you care about him, you'll put your heart on the line. For real this time. Not any half-assed, you-guys-were-both-lying-to-yourself kind of shit. Remember, he came with you to get your dog. I wasn't wild before I married, but I did my fair share of sleeping around."

Jocelyn perked up at that news and rolled her forehead on the table to look at her sister. "Really?"

Kimberly pffted. "You don't go into details like that with your baby sister."

She perked up a little more. "Now I must know."

Kimberly smiled. "Can't, because I do most of that now with hubby."

"Eww," she said and tried to smile back. She managed only a twitch of lips but it was close enough.

"Yeah. What I'm saying is, a guy that just screws you does not give a crap about you needing to pick up your dog. A man who dicks you doesn't make that voice to your dog unless he's head-over-heels in love with the dog."

She swallowed and pushed the words out, "He leaves things that he loves so that's not a good barometer."

"Huh. Interesting."

Jocelyn looked at her sister, eyes narrowed. "What is?"

"Why?"

"Doesn't think he's good enough." She blew out a frustrated breath.

"And you think he is?"

He was a bastard for the note and for not saying a proper goodbye. Completely and unequivocally. "At the moment? No. Not feeling too charitable about him leaving."

"Fair, but when you aren't so butt hurt?"

Did it make a difference? She'd shut down cold. Why would he think she gave half a crap if he stayed or went? She'd checked him off her to-do list. Yeah, she was hurt, deeply, but there was shame for how heartless she'd been. That woman existed within her and she didn't like it. Didn't like that Ian spurred that kind of response. She didn't know how to process that part yet.

"Can't." The single word was muffled by his shirt. The

one that still reeked of decadence.

"Not sure what you want me to say then, if you won't do everything to convince him he's a dumb ass for leaving what you guys had."

"I feel like the dummy. He told me the truth from the beginning. Then I got pissed when I realized he meant it. I couldn't hurt him, but I wanted to make him believe I wouldn't be heartbroken."

Her sister snorted. "If that's what you have to tell yourself to get through this, then, honey, I'm not going to say different."

Jocelyn lifted her head and banged it against the table. Hearing those words were frustrating beyond belief. Her heart told the truth though, and that meant he left. Left *them*. The sodding bastard. They both were, if she wanted to be fair and technical about it. She didn't.

That was pretty much day three.

And four.

And five.

But, by day six, she'd worked herself into a really good mad and started to pack up all his stuff to send to wherever the hell he was. Oh, she'd find him. If the mad kept rolling around like a pig in stink, she'd hunt him down and throw every piece of clothing in his face.

He'd made her unhappy. Her dog depressed. That wouldn't do at all. She needed some kind of confrontation that released some of the mad barely masking the hurt. She'd get it all out, because he'd ruined her. Rage wasn't the norm for her at all. The first few days of being depressed, exactly like her, but this uncivilized flash flood of pissed off...no. A part of her, the primitive part, embraced the honest emotion and had no shame for feeling it. And she, all of her, kind of liked it too. It felt real, alive. More so than she had since he'd left. More like how she'd felt when he was around.

Yeah, he'd probably stay gone, but they would end like they started, with a fire and fight until nothing but cinders were left. This would be the one rule they'd follow and then, maybe, she could move on.

Hopefully.

"Fucking Ian," she muttered darkly.

*****

It took Ian three days at Stanford to work up to a really good temper. A town half full of preppies, the other half with hippies and neither side had a decent pub for him to get wrecked in. Without one, all he did was yammer at the same stiff-necked professionals with more money than sense.

Once the talks were done, it was meeting after meeting to drum up business for his company. He should have been over the moon and back. Dixon Langston, the owner of the small museum, had kept his word. Doors that had been closed previously, swung open wide and the stiff-neck professionals on the other side welcomed him in.

By day four, his consultation business was booked through to the next winter. He was a success.

By day five, he didn't just have a temper but was spoiling for a good fight. The kind that broke some furniture. Maybe not, but some decent sex bruises because fighting should involve angry sex, at the least. Ian always had the name of the person he wanted to fight with right there on the edge of his mind.

She should be only a passing thought. No. Always. Right. There. Something would remind him of the way she laughed. The dewy feel of her skin after a shower. Her hair spread on her pillow while her nails dug into the soft cotton. Her. Just her. And the ever present thought of *her* drove him mad as a hatter. So much so, he finally did lose his mind.

Day six and Ian glowered at the first floor flats from his car window. He took a pull on the water, because he could taste her again. He hadn't been able to get the memory of her taste out of his mouth since he'd left. It tasted bitter twenty-four hours in. By that time he'd come to grips she wouldn't miss him.

She had his phone number. Not one shite voicemail yelling at him about leaving and not bothering to pick up his stuff. Not a single angry text message that the last exchange between them was a note about dropping off Lexxie.

Dead silence.

At that, it dawned on him, like dropping an anvil on his head. She'd been serious when she said they were done and she wouldn't be heartbroken. Then his thoughts turned to her doing that dripping-with-sex hip sway in a bar for someone else. Joce didn't care for him at all and had walked away first. Ach. Made him ache; made him mad. In cycles.

He'd come to the conclusion that if they were going to break up it was going to be ugly and very final. *El Fin.* Nothing but a complete understanding on both sides that they were done. Not cool tones that left his heart twisting in his chest.

Since he couldn't take the slow slide into insanity anymore, he'd left Stanford and went to the only place that made sense.

He slammed out the car, stomped up to Joce's door and pounded on the oak. Lexxie let out an excited yip on the other side and he could hear her nails clacking against the wood, trying to claw her way through it to get to him. Some of the mad he worked up left. Someone loved him. Someone had missed him.

Her owner opened the door and shock crossed her features. Lexxie bolted around Joce and jumped around his legs.

But then her owner's gaze narrowed to slits on him. "Oh, *Ian*. Came to say goodbye?"

"Joce," he barked back, but couldn't answer the question.

He hadn't seen her in forever. Looking at her now hit him between the eyes. She wore those silly boxers and had a jumper on. Sexy. Still. Ach. A lot of emotions crossed her face but only one stood out and it dug in his gut—lust. He'd lost himself while with her and forgot where most women wanted him—in their bed and not their heart.

Seeing that first and foremost with her had the mad roaring back easily enough. "Aye."

Her eyes widened at his tone and her mouth opened and closed. "Are *you* seriously mad at me?"

"Aye," he said again and walked past her into the flat.

The door didn't slam shut and that meant she was still levelheaded about the whole thing. Not even irritated that her discarded lover came over spoiling for a fight. He faced her and hadn't realized how close behind him she'd been. The deep, angry breath he took in dragged her scent up to him. The very definition of femininity. His fingers itched to grab hold of the jumper and drag her up to his mouth. Maybe the thought got through the anger because the lust deepened in her gaze.

"What were the rules, Ian?" The utter calmness in her voice punched him right in the heart.

"We'd fuck. You asked for your fantasies." He didn't add the last one because it had been a rule he'd thrown out, back when he thought she still cared, could care for him. Without thought, he shifted closer to her.

"I didn't break either of them, but you're angry at me?" The lust, the fire and passion blared hotter in her gaze.

"Aye."

"So why are you here? To *fuck* again?"

Ian looked away, trying to fight back the need he still had to touch her, but his dick had sprang to life the moment she'd opened the door. The cycle of ache started and added sex in to the mix. It was a wonder he wasn't in a loony bin. It felt like pure madness to be around her and worse when he wasn't.

"We both know," he said, "I stopped fucking you a long time ago."

Her breath caught and she trembled. His brain went on autopilot and, apparently, so did hers because she launched herself at him. He put out his hands to catch her and then buried his fingers in the soft jumper, pulling her closer.

No. No. Argue it out. End it. She didn't miss you; she missed your dick. But then she made a strangled, frustrated noise and lifted her arms. He yanked the jumper up, threw it across the room, and then froze. She caught his expression and whatever had propelled her to touch him vanished.

Her gaze went back to an emotion that refused to process in his mind as she stepped back. "Fine. You're angry with me. I've got some stuff for you."

It was hard for him to breathe so he answered without

thinking. "Do you now?"

She made a sound between a yell and a growl. The noise brought him up short and then Ian's gaze went back to the shirt she'd worn under the jumper and his heart tripped in his chest. Irritated to see him on her doorstep was one thing, but now he could hear it all. She sounded as pissed as he felt. Spitting mad. The kind where if you raised your voice above a certain decibel it would just turn into screaming, so you kept it low and calm. Joce was livid.

Lexxie had been sitting at the door, watching them but trotted over to him. He scooped her up. She wiggled in his arms and tried to lick his face. He pulled back, laughing softly and scratched under her neck.

"You missed me girl? I missed you. They don't make socks as warm as you." He glanced up and Jocelyn swallowed, looked away and then moved over to a box near the kitchen.

Ian frowned though he wanted to grin like a sodding idiot. "What's in the box?"

"Your things." Her words were clipped. "Was about to call you and ask you where I could send them."

"So nice of you."

She laughed. "I am, aren't I? My first urge was to burn them on the barbeque outside, but that screamed a little too much like *She-Devil* and I didn't want to come across crazy. Even though you drive me nuts sometimes."

He smiled, the fight not draining out of him because *they were going to fight*, but the ache loosened from around his heart. "And then what did you decide to do?"

"Cut them up into little pieces."

"Everything?" he asked.

"Everything you left. Including your tooth brush. Do

you want to know why? Do you want to talk?"

Since her voice was raising above the raspy calm, he put Lexxie down. The dog plopped right on his foot. "Let me have it then."

"You left, you goddamn bastard. Yes, bastard. We were dating and not *in a way*. You lived with me. We had fantastic sex. I wasn't just some lay to you. Don't lie to me. Don't you dare. You may know meaningless, but I know what more is like."

"You do know that." He kept his voice calm and knew how much madder it'd make her.

"I do," she threw at him. "And when you have it and things break, you don't just leave a note. You don't act like you can't see me when I'm across the room. You look at me with longing, goddammit."

"True."

She huffed and paced faster. "Stop agreeing with me. I want to fight. An ugly, knock-down-drag-out fight. I want to fight like we fuck. Dirty and both of us need some bruises when we walk away from this. That's who we are."

He shrugged, watching her get more riled up. After days of believing, weeks really, that Joce didn't care enough to fight with him, this was a beautiful sight. "Except when you're cooking for me."

She waved her hand. "Yeah, that's beside the point, because I am never cooking for you again. You left me. You bastard."

He stuffed his hands in his pocket. She wasn't done. Was just getting started if the flush on her face was any sign. He gave her extra fodder. "Aye. I am a dobber, but you stood in your bedroom after we did something incredible. Something that meant something out of bed and you fucking knew it. When I think on it now, I could see it as plain as day on your face, but I couldn't understand what it was before. And then—and then you gave me nothing but a cold shoulder. How dare you?"

She practically snarled at him, and he grinned. "What the hell are you smiling about? Yes, I—we—you were leaving me. How—why would I just rip my heart out and hand it to you just so you could stomp on it? *Why*?"

"Because when you love someone, you don't be daft. You let them know. Who gives a shite if they throw it back at you or walk away from you? You tell them. As fucking loudly as you can. Just so they know. That's living, Joce. Bucket list material. You walked away first and it hurt like a son of a bitch. My first. My real first. You're my bastard, Jocelyn."

He let out a breath because his heart was galloping in his chest, and she'd gone silent. "I'm not here for my clothes. I don't give a shite about them. I could buy more, but I left them with you, hoping you'd call me a bugger. Do anything. Say anything to me, but you didn't. Why?

"Ach," he said, the temper not feigned now. "Doesn't matter, because still you stand there not saying anything when you're wearing my fucking shirt."

"What?" She stopped pacing and looked down. Cambridge stretched across her high and tight breasts. She gasped and covered the words with her hands as though that would do any good.

His heart softened even more. "Did you miss me? Is that why you're wearing it?"

She sighed and met his gaze, letting her arms drop down to her sides. "It still smelled like you."

"And?" he pushed for her to question him.

She swallowed, licked her lips and finally asked, "Do you love me?"

"Aye." She ducked her head and bit her lip.

Fucking Joce. "Did I go and make you cry?"

"Yes."

"Can I kiss you now?"

She sniffed. "My dog won't let you move."

"Food," he said to Lexxie and she jumped up and toddled to the kitchen. He stepped forward and Jocelyn met him halfway.

God, he'd missed her. He buried his hands in her hair and kissed her first before anything else could be said. Or before words even bothered to show up in his head. Her fingers curled into his shirt and she kissed him back just as hard.

He pulled away only enough to look at her for what felt like the first time. "No way can I be away this long again. I'd worked myself into a good temper. And I made you wait to hear me say I love you. That puts me in the wrong."

"Ian?"

"Yeah?"

"I love you."

He grinned at her. "I knew the moment I saw the shirt."

She huffed again. "Well, pretend like you didn't and the words—"

He kissed her, hard. Again. And again. "I knew."

And then he saw when she got it. "I get wallet space."

"I get a tweed jacket. Got any single friends we can torture? I think that'll be our weekend fun."

She laughed and shook her head. "I think we can come

up with better ways to entertain ourselves. Never went out for drunken Karaoke. A tat. Was kind of busy. If you don't mind doing it all again. With me."

"I like that sound of that."

"Aye?"

"No 'r', my bonnie lass."

She grinned. "Still don't know what that means, but I love the sound it."

"We've got time." She frowned and worried her lip. "Ask," he said.

"But your business?"

"The whole goal was to get the contacts, get bigger and make a home base. Being the boss, I'm saying home is here. Because *I* can't be without *you*. If you don't want me, let me know now. I'm not the guy with words or flowers, but I will love you. If I have to leave, it's you I'm always going to come back to. And if I have to wait, I'll do it. For you."

She shook her head, tears pooling in her eyes. "You don't have to wait. There's no end date for me. Not with you."

"Aye?"

"If you miss me or I miss you, either of us can hop on a plane. Have phone sex, too. Never done that, by the way."

"No?" he asked with interest.

She shook her head again and smiled. "Couples do anything and everything to make it work because it matters." Her voice broke. "You matter to me, so much."

At that, Ian kissed her again, deeply, because he could and he needed to. She was sweet and right. Perfection. And without a doubt, he knew she loved him. Smartly, and with his heart somewhere between his throat and chest, Ian considered himself one lucky bastard.

BIO

Melissa Blue's writing career started on a typewriter one month after her son was born. This would have been an idyllic situation for a writer if it had been 1985, not 2004. Eventually she upgraded to a computer. She's still typing away on the same computer, making imaginary people fall in love.

Where to find me online:
http://www.themelissablue.com
https://www.facebook.com/AuthorOfSMR
https://twitter.com/mel_thegreat

Where to sign up for my newsletter to get updates on new releases:
http://eepurl.com/n0RR1

Special Thanks

Like all my books it's taken a village to make it presentable. So in no particular I will like to thank Suzan Butler, Sasha Delvin and Holley Trent. Aimee Duffy took the brunt of the first draft so she gets a huge, huge thanks. She also checked to make sure he sounded like a truly Dirty Scot. Last but not least, Jennifer Leeland who not only read the second draft, but listened to me whine for months about this book. I can't thank any of you enough.

Shawna Guzman, the editor of many of my books, gets her own paragraph in this thanks. She knows why.

Anything wonky in this story falls squarely on my shoulders. They tried. They really did try.

Other Titles by Melissa Blue

Her Insatiable Scot, Under The Kilt

Keri Pearson is currently between jobs, so there's nothing to lose when her cousin promises her a glowing recommendation from a top expert in their field in exchange for a small favor. All she has to do is lie about who she is and pretend to be married to a charming Scot for three hours. Her sexy-as-hell pretend husband makes it too easy to play the part of newlyweds. The last thing she should do is trust him or the genuineness of his lust or adoration, but his touch ignites an unexpected desire.

Tristan Baird turned his back on his past with plenty of regrets, but when his brother blackmails him, Tristan can't say no. Given his brother saved his neck, an afternoon doing what he does best doesn't seem like too much to ask. And it's for a good cause. Doing the job right guarantees his brother and new wife will have the home of their dreams. But his stunning accomplice complicates the job. She is everything he always wanted and couldn't have. The kind of woman who is too smart to ever trust a former conman.

The three-hour commitment stretches into five sexually charged days as they fight the explosive connection. As each day passes, Keri must remind herself what is true and what is false, but the lines are blurring. Tristan can only hope his past doesn't come back to ruin their future.

Kilted For Pleasure, Under The Kilt

Callan Baird used to laugh more than he frowned, but that was before his wife died. Now his life is duty, debts and a general apathy for anything else. And then Victoria Burke burst into his life. She's everything he wants to corrupt.

Victoria has two choices: agree to a grouchy, sexy Scotsman's extortion or call her boss to explain why she can't do her job. Since she's spent the last three years rebuilding her career as antique appraiser, and this one commission could make or break it, the decision is a no-brainer. Except everything about Callan is complicated.

He sees no problem turning their work relationship into a sexual one. She refuses to break her boss' no-fraternization rule. He's the one thing she wants and the one thing she can't have. He's had his one great love, and doesn't want a replacement. His heart doesn't agree, because she's everything he desires.

Callan will have to let go of his past if he wants Victoria to be in his future.

Weekend Lover, Down With Cupid Shorts series

The weekend that started it all...

Sebastian Clark's intentions are simply to buy Nicole, a beautiful stranger, a drink, make her laugh and disappear before dawn. As a publicist for *Snapshot*, his days are long and his moral code is to always keep things light. Until he touches her and lust fades any lasting hold on common sense. His questionable motives pave a road to unbelievable pleasure.

Nicole Harrison is on the fast track for a promotion at *Limelight*, a PR boutique. She's given up dating, especially handsome men. They tend to suck up time and sometimes common sense. Sebastian has the ability to do both. One single night won't break her own rules and Nicole gives in to temptation.

The boundaries are clear—no last names, no shared details. She has only to walk away to end the affair. One night turns into three, and her naughty little weekend becomes more than just sex.

One night of consenting pleasure sets Sebastian Clark and Nicole Harrison on a course that could ultimately destroy them both, or bring them a love for all time...

Down With Cupid, Down With Cupid Shorts series

Two months after a weekend of forbidden pleasure should have been more than enough time for Nicole Harrison to forget Sebastian's charming smiles and wicked kisses. During those nights together, Nicole temporarily left behind her driven lifestyle as a publicist and took what she wanted, experiencing freedom and the wild abandon of their reckless agreement. And that's the hardest part to erase from her memory.

Unfortunately, one detail was tantamount—Sebastian Clark is a publicist and now he's gunning for her job.

Sebastian never allows himself to get tangled in knots by a woman, and, yet, he can't stop dreaming about Nicole's silky thighs and ripe lips, how she'd shuddered under his touch. He doesn't need a woman who is more of a shark than he when it comes to PR, except he's seen every, single soft inch of her. Now they'll have to work side by side and somehow ignore what feels like unfinished business.

Will the weekend they spent together turn out to be more than they could have ever imagined, or will past hurts and career ambitions stand in their way? Only Cupid knows...

You find my full backlist on my website:
http://www.themelissablue.com

Excerpt from Her Insatiable Scot

Tristan Baird glanced at his hand and hoped he'd have a different reaction this time. The simple gold wedding band gleamed in the soft spring sunlight. His chest tightened, and he had the sudden urge to chop off his ring finger.

Aye. The same reaction he had the first twenty times. If he wasn't waiting for his fake wife he'd have let his mind wander. Nothing but shite thoughts if the first one involved sawing off an appendage.

The purr of an engine dragged his mind and gaze to the parking lot's entrance. A cherry-red roadster pulled up beside him. The windows were tinted. His neck tingled. Likely his fake wife for the afternoon.

The things we do for family.

The car door opened, and that sour thought got drowned in a pool of lust. From a leg. An unbelievably skyscraper-high heel stepped out of the car. Yes, a woman was attached to it, but he needed a minute to take in the foot and shoe. *Dainty* wasn't a word he'd normally use, but it fit. He flexed the offending hand with the ring and imagined he'd likely shatter her arch if he were to ever get a good grasp of her ankle, or nip at her heel to see if she'd shudder and moan.

His gaze rose and stalled at the hint of thigh. Even the indentation of muscle looked tenuous, but there he could see her legs tightening around him, her hips a blur of curves as she slapped her arse back down on him. Those hips he'd have remembered from the wedding.

Then again he'd been smashed. His little brother had let a woman wrap him into knots, enough so he'd let himself get talked into marriage. A smile broke through Tristan's frown.

Just like the good old days when it was just him, Ian and their Da, they made their way through a bottle of Scotch. This one had been vintage and highbrow, but passable in the scheme of things. Much to his surprise, Ian's wife, Joce, had drunk a good lot herself. Probably didn't make much for a wedding night, or morning for that matter.

Yet Tristan would have remembered *this* woman through a fuzz of Scotch. He crossed his arms, leaned against the car and waited for the rest of her. Full breasts, sharp chin, plump lips, honey-brown skin and dark brown eyes.

Nothing about her jolted his memory other than she looked a little like Joce around the eyes and nose. Her bangs stopped at her ebony-shaded brows. The bob kissed her sharp jawline. If she'd been at the wedding and he couldn't remember her, then he'd chew a leather hat as penance.

"Tristan, I'm guessing," she said and shut the car door.

Her husky voice made him straighten, but his eyes narrowed. She had tried to sound bored but nerves had filtered in. American through and through. If nothing else about her stuck with him, her voice definitely would have.

Curious, he dug in his pocket for the trinket he'd plucked out of his luggage before heading over to the hotel. “Nice to meet you. Keri?” At her nod, he added, “And I know this may sound forward, but here's your wedding ring.”

She snorted and put her hand out. “The shit we do for family.”

He chuckled, finally relaxing, but held on to the ring box. If he let himself think too hard about the bauble, he'd change his mind about handing it over. Maybe when he had picked up his gold wedding band from the pawn shop, he should have bought a different ring for her too.

He had this gem for a long while, tucked away, but not forgotten. Three large stones, a princess cut, and the ring was immaculate. The ring was supposed to mean... He grimaced. Now he was turning morose.

Glancing at Keri, he brushed aside the thoughts. Maybe the next few hours wouldn't be complete shite. “What'd you get bribed with?” he asked.

“First Jocelyn started with 'I wish you could have made it to the wedding.' Yeah, I told her last minute I had to work after sending my RSVP. I'm not good at dealing with people, but you'd think she'd have led with something else. She went for the jugular. No offense, but that husband of hers made her ruthless.”

Given he'd taught his brother all the ways to be cutthroat when he wanted what he wanted, Tristan let the dig pass. “And then?”

“She lulled me into complacency with small talk until I didn't feel guilty at all anymore. Then she hit me between the eyes. 'I need a huge favor. One so big I'll pay you.' By the end of the conversation I was going to get a damn good recommendation from *Ian Baird* because my cousin could vouch for my conservator work, especially the scientific research. How exactly could I say no? They are on their honeymoon. Who wants to go to a required class on their honeymoon? Hell, they're not even in the country." She blinked as though surprised she'd let all those words loose into the world. "You?"

He owed his brother for keeping him out of jail. When Ian asked him to break a promise he'd made to himself, he'd agreed. He still felt conflicted about even being here and what he was asked to do, but Tristan had never evened the scales between himself and Ian. But he didn't suffer from the same problem with rambling. He dropped the box into her palm. "He's my brother."

She clicked it open and her eyes widened. "This is fake, right?"

He raised a brow, surprised she couldn't tell. She apparently knew relics, antiques but not jewelry. Before showing up he'd braced himself for questions. Where did he get the ring? Who did it belong to? What happened to that relationship? Why would you give this to *me*? If he could avoid that sordid tale, he would. If all they were going to do was spend a few hours in each other's life, he didn't want to rip open a wound that would never fully heal.

"Aye."

She gasped and then laughed. "You guys actually say that?"

Despite the dour mood wanting to descend, he laughed too. "Aye." He infused more Scot into his tone.

She slipped on the ring. "My cousin was screwed from the word 'go.'" A frown started to crease her brows. "Are you sure this is fake? Feels real."

The dress she wore caught on the breeze scented with

the hint of ocean. There was a flash of her smooth brown legs until the wind died down. He could get behind California weather. No jewelry graced her wrists or neck and her earlobes were free of any holes. Now he frowned. He couldn't remember the last woman he'd ever met who didn't even wear earrings occasionally.

Since she wouldn't know the difference with the ring, that meant he wouldn't have to explain where he got it from—basically he could keep his past to himself. Tristan answered again with, "Aye."

He notched his head to the hotel. They had quite a bit to go to get to the entrance. Only a little after three in the afternoon and the parking lot barely had any spaces left. The historical society association or whatever they called themselves required all applicants to take a course. It was their way to vet serious historical home owners. Ian and Joce couldn't make this convention and the next one wouldn't be for another year. If all these people were here for that class, then his brother and sister-in-law's insistence for him and Keri to show up made sense.

He dug in his other pocket and handed her the clip-on badge he'd found in the first drawer by the refrigerator in Joce's flat. Thanks to it and the registration papers no one would ask for their ID.

"Thanks." She faced the hotel. "Okay. How are we going to pull this off?"

"I know enough about Scottish history and my brother's consulting business to fake any answers. Anything technical I'll punt to you."

Her mouth pinched into a thin line. "We don't exactly look like Ian and Jocelyn."

He shrugged. "Change blindness should cover the rest.

The next time these folks take a gander at Mr. and Mrs. Baird, they'll barely recall I was taller and stockier. You must have changed your hair. Just avoid any pictures and the rest should be fine."

She gave him a dubious glance. "You've heard of the change blindness theory?"

He didn't feel offense at the question. He didn't look the sort of man who trolled scientific journals or even YouTube videos. "Who hasn't?"

She waved her hand. "I was talking about the married thing. Two weeks and we should still be on our honeymoon. I met you three minutes ago. I don't think we can fake love and forever."

Tristan thought on the problem for a split second. "I'll put my hand on your arse every five minutes and that should settle that."

She blinked. "You're serious."

He grinned at her. "As a heart attack."

She pursed her lips, inspected him from top to bottom. Her eyes darkened before she smiled back at him. "Okay."

His grin slipped, because he'd been screwing with her. She didn't give him time to reply but walked forward. Her hips swayed, lifting the dress up midthigh with each step. He forgot about joking, because he wanted an excuse to put his hands on her arse every five minutes.

Shaking his head, he took three long strides to catch up. He hesitated for a moment and then grasped her hand. He ran a finger down the curve of her thumb—he couldn't help it. Her hand was just as dainty, feminine.

She stopped, whirling to face him. "What are you doing?"

"Molesting your hand." He took a step forward, but

she refused to move. "I would apologize, but you never know who is watching."

Her gaze whipped around the parking lot. Fortunately for him folks milled about while others headed toward the entrance.

She pinned him with a stare. "You do look like an ass grabber. So, you caught me off guard with the hand holding."

He tried to keep the laugh out of his voice. "We do have to sell this."

She stepped into his space the way he just had into hers. Her leg brushed along the inside of his thigh. His cocked tightened. She placed a hand on his stomach. Heat burned in his chest and then she smiled up at him, a gleam in her eye. His heart thudded in anticipation. Oh, he didn't think she'd kiss him or anything that he'd love to happen, but he was curious to know how she'd react. If honest, he could admit he was testing her to see how much fun they could have.

"So"—she lowered her voice—"we have a deal, then? You grab my ass every five minutes and I'll..." She licked her lips, her lids growing heavy. "Touch something of yours."

He wrapped his hand around hers and placed their joined hands on his chest. Her fingers had a slight tremble, but she kept her face devoid of any nervousness. She had one hell of a bluff. That turned him on more than anything else about her. Folks walked by them, looking away just as quickly from what appeared to be an intimate moment between a loving couple.

But now Tristan knew he'd get as far as she'd let him go. Headstrong but adventurous? He could have fun with that.

Finally, he said, "Sounds like a deal."

She laughed, the husky sound spilling over him. "The next few hours are going to be fun, but just to be clear, if you do grab my ass, I'll break your hand."

"Auch," he scoffed. "Woman, it was a joke."

"That's not what your eyes said."

He met and held her gaze "Probably not. You're an attractive woman, but that's beside the point. Due to bribery and blackmail, we're spending an afternoon together listening to someone blather on about preservation of a historical home, of all dull subjects. I'd rather someone wax my nads. If flirting with you would make this afternoon less shite, then I'm all for it."

"You flirt with your hands?"

He liked her. Really, he did. "There's another way?" Since she hadn't moved, he pressed his free hand to her waist, bringing her flush against him.

To his surprise, she looked flustered for a second. "Tristan, my cousin warned me about you. I thought she was full of it."

He smiled again, loosening his hold on her only slightly. "I'm sure my brother gave her the rundown, and then she met me at the wedding."

She put both hands on his chest and pushed him back, breaking all physical contact they had. "Either way, strictly hand holding."

"I swear on my honor." Tristan didn't add he didn't have any, but her brow lift negated the need to say it.

She put out her hand. "Let's try this again and see how long before you try for more."

He wrapped his fingers around hers. Her palm was

warm and slightly damp. Once again her reaction conflicted with her words and demeanor. Interesting. He'd conned a lot of people in his lifetime. A lot of women. He rolled his shoulders to shift the weight of wrongs.

This woman puzzled him, though. His brother had been clear that this foray into his life would be quick and required very little. In short, Tristan couldn't fuck up. He'd pretend to be his brother for a few hours. Play nice with Jocelyn's cousin and not let the door hit him in the arse on his way back out of Ian's life.

He owed his brother that much, but as he looked at the woman beside him, other ideas started to take hold. Not like his brother would be surprised that they had, but it was a few hours at the most. Not much could happen...so he'd try to have all the fun he could.

End of Excerpt

Made in the USA
Columbia, SC
01 June 2018